Original title
"ΟΤΑΝ Ο ΑΝΕΜΟΣ ΦΥΣΗΞΕΙ ΑΝΤΙΘΕΤΑ"

"WHEN THE WIND BLOWS AGAINST"

Translation: Chris Cal
Editor: Tommy Gales
Cover page: Panos Chatzieleftheriou
Typesetting: Jason McKinney

OLEANDER BOOKS
Griva Digeni 2
17342 - Athens
Greece
info@oleanderbooks.com
Site: oleanderbooks.com

ISBN: 978-618-87954-1-9

Panos Chatzieleftheriou

WHEN THE WIND BLOWS AGAINST

A FEW WORDS ABOUT THE BOOK

"When the Wind Blows Against" is a book based on actual events, dedicated to those who managed to be themselves, even when the people around them could not stand it. It is the story of a boy who grew up on the social margins in a village in Mani in the 50s-60s.

He was born a "stranger" in his own home, but he learned to endure violence, rejection, and loss. A journey from the darkness that marked his youth to the definitive change that he believed would set him free. But even then, his heart refused to be silent.

His personal struggle is a hymn to diversity and the power of truth. With body and soul scarred by violence, friendship sacrificed, but also by the love that always returns, he becomes a symbol of courage for those who dare to be true.

Panos Chatzieleftheriou

CHAPTER ONE

WHEN THE WIND BLOWS AGAINST

Reminiscing

The iron beams rusted, along with the supports that held the wooden planks of the pier. The saltiness does not know how to forgive; it resembles a woodworm that eats insatiably whatever it finds in its path. The planks were indifferent to their fate; you could say they were willfully blind. They believed, the fools, that nothing could break them. They laughed and mocked the wave when it crashed against them with force.

"Aren't you tired of going back and forth? You're tiring yourself for nothing," they would tell him.

Once, the wave became very angry with their disrespect. So, it secretly made a deal with the winds and time.

The Mistral and the Sirocco took action. They grew so strong that they forced the planks to hit each other like walnut shells.

In the end, they could not stand it; they became rotten wooden carcasses, leaning haphazardly on one another, abandoned to decay. Little did they know, the unfortunate ones, that nothing can resist the touch of time and the power of the sea.

Even the stones that supported the pier were overgrown with grass; stones that had been piled up by men on their backs, pouring rivers of sweat, and which were now filled with crabs, barnacles, and slippery algae. The little fishes had set up a whole colony.

The old days were a picture of life complete; now it has faded. Gone are the schooners whose captains tied their sturdy hulls to the pier, to the thick ropes. Gone are the large fishing boats that reached as far as Tunisia and the Barbary Coast. Gone are the sailors who strolled around in the arms of the elderly prostitute they had shopped for earlier in a tavern.

Only the wind carried to the ears of the moonstruck one the echo of shouts cursing the assistants to load the goods or the loot from the piracy quickly. Perhaps the dreamer's gaze could distinguish shadows from the few ragged, drunken beggars, who, on their knees, begged for a few pennies, just enough to drink their dram.

Absolute abandonment with a salty taste; a shocking confirmation that nothing ever stays the same. Only one hundred and sixty souls were left in Gerolimenas to perpetuate the memories of the greatness that had passed. Traveled by word-of-mouth, the stories of the pier were passed on to the generations that followed, until today.

The Little Maniots

Two young Mani boys usually chose this old, dilapidated pier to spend their afternoons fishing. There was no need for school; Areopolis was too far away for their short legs; where could they go?

Sunburned, in tattered shorts and soiled T-shirts, they splashed their blackened feet in the calm sea. They held a long, crooked wooden reed in their hands and tried to trick the cunning little fish with dead worms. But time passed, without catching a single fish; it was getting dark, and they had to return.

If they stayed late after sunset, they risked their ears; their Maniot mothers had no qualms about plucking them out.

Paul, with a long, drawn-out "ugh - I'm bored," broke the silence.

Full of nerves and frustration, he hit the reed on his knee, broke it in two, and threw it with force onto the rocks.

"They don't eat, the little devils, George; it's like they've been hiding? I saw Bathrelos with his sons here the other day; they were holding dynamites in their hands. Look how far they've come! Wherever they go, they leave nothing behind; they even kill the little ones! Now I've got an idea. It's not about fishing; what do you say, we go up to the terraces tomorrow morning?"

"And what should we do, Pavlakas, on the dry stone paths and the aspalathos plants?"

"We'll go, you fool, higher up, we'll climb to the threshing floor behind the lamppost. There, we'll stick lime-twigs into the dry wild grass to catch some birds. Hey, should we call Dimitros to come over?"

"Don't count on him; he says he'll come, but he stays behind."

"As if you're right, George; I heard his mother say in her coffee that he's constantly helping his mother with the laundry, the dry frying, the housework; he doesn't even go fishing with his old man. The other day, he started crying, and Tzanis threw him off the boat; the coward almost drowned."

"Come on, Paul, the scoundrel is a sissy. Walks like a gang hit, talks like a gang hit. Lately, wherever you look for him, wherever you find him, he's been playing with her sister's doll. The other day, when I went there, I caught him changing a doll's dress. We'll go anyway; I'll bring the slingshot with me, for some turtledoves; finally, these birds have appeared. As soon as the first light breaks, I'll wait for you at the collapsed bridge!"

Mani, A Harsh Place Full Of Magic

To the right of Gerolimenas, letting your gaze wander openly towards it, it is clearly visible that the sun is always sad when it leaves Mani.

Its last weak rays stretch to the cape and even further. They look, in the undulating dark blue sea, like thousands of orange-yellow, rare diamonds. It is as if they are small, bright boats slowly getting lost in their ride. On land, the fading sun does not frighten the proud stone towers that are darkening; they know well that the moon has a way of reviving their magnificence.

The 'Holy Port' on the Apagian Gulf, with its turquoise waters, was once a stronghold of cruel pirates, adventurers, and merchants. Its rugged tip fades into Cape Tainaro. An old lighthouse there, all night long, tirelessly sent a bright message to the ships entering and leaving the Mediterranean. And if some exhausted captain threw his boat onto the rocks, then the bell in the stone-built church of Agios Nikolaos would toll. And the people of Mani ran for help.

The Maniots are unruly people; hard-nosed, watered

with wine from dry vines and water from the springs of Taygetos, the backbone of Mani.

Mani is a magical place; once you go there, you are hooked. But when the wind blows the opposite way in this place, then...

Dimitros

Paul, George, Dimitros, and two or three other kids, in their shorts, gathered one Sunday morning, after church, in a dirt field in Gerolimenas to play with their "Capitol" marbles. They dug five small holes in the ground: four around the perimeter, one in the center. When one of them managed to put his marble into all of them in one go, leaving the one in the center last, without missing, he won! They let Dimitros be the last in line to try. They knew, clumsy as he was, that he wouldn't be able to do it, since, no matter how many times he tried, he threw his marble so severely that he provoked the laughter and teasing of his friends. Then his red cheeks would turn even redder - from shame. The rejection he felt from his friends and the disappointment in himself were so great that he would run away to hide in his mother's arms.

Chiona, like a mother wolf, always opened her arms lovingly to welcome him. She wiped the tears from his wet cheeks and comforted him:

"It doesn't matter," she would say, "in another game, you'll see, you'll be the best."

"I don't want to play with them, Mom, they're always making fun of me," he would answer. "I want to sit here with you at home, help you. And if you don't have any chores, it's okay, I'll play with our little Anna."

Chiona, the mother of Dimitros and Anna, is the literate one of the family. She had finished elementary school and two or three grades in high school; Chiona was a real sweetheart, brilliant, and tender with her children, but a wolf to all the others. She was not afraid of Tzanis or anyone else. A tough woman, she managed everything on her own, her offspring, her husband; no one lacked anything; she even went to the fields and supported her husband's work. Crown!

Neither on the way to nor on the way back to school in Areopolis did anyone walk next to Dimitros. He held his younger sister's hand tightly, and they walked together. In class, he sat alone at the first desk; the other children avoided sitting next to him, as if he were a leper. There were times when they jokingly called him "Mitsoula", a girly name.

What if the old maid teacher, with her high bun and her crooked legs, punished the troublemakers? Their open palms were turned into beets by the ruler. But in vain, did the same after a while.

It was complicated in those years for a Maniot child to have a confused personality. For the girls, fate was predetermined; no one was spared. But for the boys who did not follow in their father's footsteps, it was something tragic.

Dimitros did not hide his nature from the first years of his life. And why should he? Did he understand? The cloudy mirror did not reveal the soul. He never hid what made him happy.

In the carefreeness of his carefree childhood, how was it possible for him to understand the future consequences of his difference?

A truth of his own, which became a poisonous sting in his father's wounded ego. There were not a few times when the insults about Dimitros in the tavern and the coffee shop left him speechless, with his head bowed.

On October 26, on the feast of Saint Demetrius, in the café, a fellow villager said to him, speaking loudly:

"Hey Tzanis, happy nameday to your little Demeter; come on, treat us now!"

"May the Charon reward you, you excommunicated. Now wait, and I will show you the reward."

He pulled the double-edged blade from his belt and rushed like a raging bull to slaughter him like a lamb. He barely managed to seriously wound him before the patrons took the knife from his hand. For three days, he hid, sleepless, in the mountains like a thief, lest the gendarmes arrest him. He returned when things calmed down, but he started a vendetta that lasted for a few years. Fortunately, it did not cost any human lives.

The family's father, Tzanis, is the respected husband of Mom Chiona. Tall, burly, with a rough expression that reminded you of a Sicilian mafioso. He knew everything, not even an ant on his feet escaped him. He was often so abrupt in conversation that he instilled fear in you. The difficult survival, the post-war years, and the hard dealings with the port merchants had turned him into an unyielding stone. He became a well-known oil merchant, with his own olive press, and sent virgin olive oil throughout the Peloponnese.

Dimitros' godly grandmother knew a priest from Lagia who served from time to time at a small church in Kato Boularioi. Whenever she found a peasant, she would go up and come. So she told him that she wanted to meet him. When she saw him, she told him everything about her grandson so that he would bless him, and the curse would leave him. However, one afternoon, a peasant caught the priest touching the young boy's immature body in the church sanctuary. They excommunicated the priest; The crowd almost lynched him. The stigma, however, remained hanging over the small community, further infecting Dimitros' already open wound.

It's not the identity of a person's soul that counts; it's the actions that characterize it that count, even if he does not cause them. You see, it's these mishaps of nature, where God puts the wrong souls in the wrong bodies.

Often, the father's wounded ego would hold his own child responsible for the humiliation. Then his anger would burst out on the child's flesh, which would tear when the leather strip reached the end of its path. Whenever the mother intervened to save him from his furious hands, all he could do was hit her too, saying to her:

"It's your fault that my rifle became a fagot. I've disgraced myself in all of Mani! Take him and go to hell, do you hear?"

The next morning, he would calm down and apologize to his wife. However, when he came home drunk the next night or, at most, the day after that, the same scenario would play out.

Dimitros liked to paint. His uncle, Sampatis, Chiona's brother, was the richest in the family; he was a ship's captain. On every leave, when he returned to Mani, he would bring him drawing pads, pencils, and watercolors. He brought him many things; he loved Dimitros and didn't care what they said.

The little boy would jump for joy when he received the gifts. He would hide them reverently in the trunk of the bedroom, under the blankets. On quiet nights, when there was no noise in the stone house, when everyone else was asleep, he would secretly take the oil lamp and place it next to him. He would rest his back on the headboard and, with the pad fixed to his bony knees, he would draw all night.

His own world was different; there was no room for violence, rejection, or coercion there. There was love in his colors, there was forgiveness.

The landscapes he painted had a clear sky, a bright sun, a bright moon, shining stars, and smiling flowers. He didn't paint people; he didn't want to. He only drew the priest one day with horns, a tail, and scarlet robes. Around him were flames and faint, hard human figures burning in them.

Here and there, he showed his paintings to little Anna; he trusted only her.

He loved her very much, and she loved him too. When Tzanis beat him, he would hide under her bed. She couldn't bear to see and hear her brother's pain.

◆ ◆ ◆

One morning, his father forced him to go fishing with him.

Scared, Dimitros, unable to refuse, followed him; he was only twelve years old at the time. The strong Ponente stunned the inexperienced little boy, and he had difficulty standing in the boat. Tzanis, seeing him in this mess, without hesitation, caught him like a rag and threw him into the sea. Dimitros almost drowned. No one will ever know why, after a while, Tzanis picked him up in the boat. No one knows whether he did it out of compassion for his child or because he did not want to stand before the angry Maniot mother and the bench of the law. Only he knew.

From Mani To The Capital

As soon as they left Tripoli, the heavy raindrops had set up a barricade for them. The raindrops fell incessantly, making a noise on the heavy sheet metal.

The back and forth of the windshield wipers resembled the slow steps of a poor man struggling to stay upright. With great difficulty, the wipers managed to keep the windshield clean. Their annoying, long-drawn-out squeak accompanied the aged sound of the engine of the tired Opel, which was struggling to climb the narrow slopes of Achladokambos.

Suddenly, a heavy dusk fell, like most of February, when you don't know where or how it will end. In a few minutes, the gray-black sky and the fog gave you the impression that the clouds were paying a visit to the earth. They brought gifts: the furious wind that raged, the heavy rain, the lightning, and the thunder.

Tzanis, to be able to see in the haze, had his face almost glued to the window. He gripped the steering wheel, cursing - between his teeth - any Saint he knew. He hoped, with the curses, to hit one of the Saints in the head, to make him afraid. Maybe then, he would take advantage of the bad weather that had set out to torment them.

When they set off, shortly after noon, from Gerolimenas to ascend to the capital, it was a blessing in disguise; there wasn't a cloud on the horizon. Okay, there was a bit of wind, to put it mildly, but that was all. Besides, in Mani, the winds are permanent; they drop anchor there even in the middle of summer. They expected to reach the new house they had rented in Kypseli without any problems by early evening.

The decision to permanently abandon Laconia was not easy. But come on, there was no other way.

Chiona, his crown, in the passenger seat, didn't say a word; she was terrified. With her legs drawn close to the seat, she gripped the leather door handle tightly with her right hand and, with her left, clumsily tried to clean the fogged-up windshield with a piece of cloth.

Dimitros was a handsome, melancholy fifteen-year-old boy with thick, curly black hair and large, expressive black eyes. He rested his head against the glass of the car door, sadness etched across his face. He didn't speak; he only stared at the rain, his gaze directed to the side as he sat in the back seat. He attempted to count the thick drops that descended from the sky, tragically ending their short journey as they fell against the lifeless glass.

This uprooting from his homeland for his parents was pain, a curse; but for him, freedom and redemption. He was not afraid of bad weather at all.

He was frightened by the memories of the humiliation, the violence, and the degrading behavior that he had received from the moment he began to understand his life. Yes, they sowed an unbridgeable void in his troubled soul.

The further they moved away, the more he rejoiced. The soil of Mani did not accommodate the "different". The sharp blade of public opinion cut off their acquired right to live in the place they loved. His younger sister, Anna, stayed behind in the village until she finished her grade. She would later come to Athens with her uncle, Sampatis, her mother's brother.

"My Dimitros, are you okay?" Chiona asked, without looking at him.

"Yes, mother, I'm okay," he replied, without taking his gaze from the window.

"How could it not be?" Tzanis added angrily, casting a glance at his wife. "We left home for his sake. I want to see his progress in Athens. This time, he won't escape me; if he doesn't keep his dirty laundry hidden, I'll slaughter him like a goat on my knee."

The harsh words broke Dimitros' heart. Once again, fear raped every cell of his body. Like a beaten dog, he squirmed, trembling, in the back seat of the car.

"You're not talking, are you? You're not saying anything?" Tzanis asked him.

"Whatever I say, my father, you won't listen to it," he replied, misty.

"Why won't I listen to it, huh? Am I deaf?"

"I didn't say that, no. I'm just saying what I am is not what I want for myself!"

And he burst into sobs; sobs drawn from the depths of a blackened soul, so that they would be mixed with the rain and the wind, and lost with them.

Seeing that the situation was getting out of hand, Chiona cleverly spoke up:

"We have time for this, my lord," she said, and patted him on the head tenderly.

He looked at her, clearly enraged, muttered something through his teeth, and then fell silent.

The sudden storm did not last long; after it had done its thing, it died down. Like everything, nothing lasts long, nothing lasts forever. Even hope, once it becomes reality, goes into the time crypt of memories.

They passed Saint Vasilis and Chiliomodi, without exchanging another word. They had less than thirty kilometers left before they reached the National Road.

A small café, one of those you used to find on provincial roads, allowed them to rest. There, they would serve the weary travelers coffee, soft drinks, and local delicacies. Inside, you could see, on old shelves, small tin boxes with all sorts of spoon sweets; perhaps even a forgotten counter in a corner, with bags of noodles and tarhana, handmade by the goldhand village woman.

The wooden door of the café had swollen at the bottom from the humidity, and Tzanis was forced to push it hard to open it. There was no one in the small shop except the bony middle-aged café owner, who jumped out of his chair like a spring as soon as he saw them, or instead heard them, when they entered his café. He had fixed his elbow, to be safe, on the marble table to support his head, while he slept, your good friend, of the good weather. Unkempt, dry-skinned, with a scraggly mustache and a dirty short apron, he woke up abruptly from the door slamming and stood up, tall as a stork, to welcome them.

"Welcome, welcome! The weather didn't let anyone in today. Not a soul has set foot here since noon. Sit wherever you like."

"Good evening. Two coffees and an orangeade. Please, hurry up, we are late."

"Right away! Ah! My lady has made some local cheese pie. Do you want one?"

"Father, I'm very hungry; can I please have a piece?"

"You shut up, you wretch; you'll eat when we get to town. Be patient."

"But… "

Before Dimitros could say another word, Tzanis' palm fell on his face like a lightning bolt, with such force that it almost fell along with the chair.

"I don't want the coffee," said Chiona, fuming, looking at him angrily.

She grabbed Dimitros by the hand, pulling him sharply, and they returned to the car.

Tzanis didn't move from his seat; he only turned his gaze to the coffee shop owner, who was looking at him in bewilderment.

"What are you looking at, you lazy? Go ahead and bring me some coffee, do you hear? We're late, I'm telling you!"

"Yes, sir! I'll be right back."

In the car, Dimitros was inconsolable; Chiona had sat

in the back seat with him, holding him in her arms. She was gently tangling her fingers in his curly hair, letting tears stream down her cheeks.

"What did I do, mother? What did I do?" Dimitros shouted, crying and clearly indignant. "I was very hungry and asked for a piece of cheese pie. Is it wrong? I can't stand it anymore; he beats me, curses me, as if I were a dog. One day I will kill him, you'll see."

"Don't say such things, my Dimitros. Everything will be okay in Athens."

The Apartment In Kypseli

A few hours later, the heavy car stopped outside a four-story apartment building in Kypseli. It was past nine. Tzanis opened the heavy door of the Opel and stood for a moment outside the car. First, he stretched his arms out to the side, then he rubbed his buttocks vigorously.

"My ass got caught in this wreck. Come on, move your feet, and let's unload."

Fortunately for them, the apartment was on the ground floor. A few suitcases and three or four bags of blankets were all that were unloaded. Whatever they left behind in Mani would be brought the next day by a close relative of Chiona in his truck.

As soon as he stepped onto the dirty asphalt, Dimitros was with his mouth wide open. Motionless, speechless, he inhaled fresh images of polluted air. His immature mind could not comprehend what his sad eyes were seeing. Here, there were no dark towers or a vast sea. Here, there were multi-story concrete boxes full of lights, muddy water that flowed hastily to hide in the sewers, blurry shadows of people who were lost in nowhere.

All he knew was from some old, scattered photographs. He had never been to the city. He had never ventured further from his hometown.

The apartment they bought had been furnished with all the comforts. Chiona would go back and forth for several days by bus from Gerolimenas to Athens, like a bee from flowers to a hive, until she had it tidied up. The Maniot women were tireless, taking all the burden on themselves; strong bodies! They always found a way to get what they wanted. They called them the "crowns" of the family; their right was a mountain. The men thought that they had the controls. In their dreams!

The idea to start their life again in the capital was clearly hers. She wanted to protect her child, but her hopes had vanished in Mani, and the turmoil had become great. Tzanis didn't even want to hear about leaving his place! What do you say, we'll run away? He cursed gods and demons, threatened to burn them alive. However, the great shame he felt and Chiona's insistence that they leave softened him a little; now they found themselves in Kypseli, trying to pack up their new home.

The two minor bedrooms faced the open space. On the facade, a modest living room was lit by a narrow French window that led to a balcony a span long. Kitchen, bathroom, and that was all. For Dimitros? Greatness!

He would share an entire bedroom with his sister. A new bed, a bedside table with a lamp, a wardrobe, a desk, not even in his wildest dreams had he imagined such luxury. What to do with old Mani with crags, he thought. Here he had it all: no one knew him, no one would make fun of him, no one would laugh at him anymore.

With these thoughts and a secret smile, he surrendered himself to Morpheus's embrace on his first night in Athens, while Chiona tenderly covered him with the blanket, kissing him on the forehead.

It had not yet dawned when his mother and father sat down at the small square kitchen table to drink their morning coffee. The new environment, to say the least, was stifling; absolutely nothing to do with the kitchen of their tower, from where, looking out the window, you could see the sea of Gerolimenas.

They were discussing what would happen to Dimitros. There was no way they would accept him into any school - the school year would end in just three months. Besides, he had missed many classes. In January, they had to permanently stop him from attending Areopolis High School. The reason was an incident in the toilets, when some of his classmates cornered him in one of them. They tore his pants, stripped him, took his underwear, and wrote "fag" on it with his name underneath. Then they tied it with a string and hung it on the courtyard door. Dimitros became a public figure throughout Mani. He wrapped himself in an old sack from a nearby grocery store, ashamed, so that he could return home.

The troublemakers, of course, were caught and expelled. So what? The atmosphere worsened day by day. From then on, he remained locked up in the house until noon on the day they left for Athens. He didn't even dare to appear in the yard; everyone laughed at him. The mocking comments were given and taken, so much so that his mother was forced to fight with the neighbors — they even got into fights.

Shame, gossip, fights, it was no longer possible to keep going. Disheartened, with their hands on their hearts, they made the big decision to leave Mani.

At Nikolas' House

A second cousin of Tzanis, Nikolas, the son of a first cousin of his mother, had lived in Maniatika, a district of Piraeus, since his childhood. They were the same age and played together as children until his parents took him and moved to the capital. He was now a well-known photographer in the area with his own photo studio in Thiseio, Athens. So, until they saw what would happen next year with school, they thought about talking to him to see if they could get Dimitros to learn at least a craft.

Without wasting any time, that same morning, with Chiona's consent, he called him on the phone. The receiver rang three times, but it didn't get a fourth.

"Come on, who is it?"

"Come on, Nikolas, good morning. It's your cousin, Tzanis!"

"Where are you, you old-timer? We've been lost! I haven't heard from you for years and years. What are you doing? The family? Is everyone okay?"

"Everything is fine, cousin. But I want to meet, to talk in person. Our family arrived in Athens yesterday permanently, and I want your help."

"With pleasure, cousin, if I can. When do you want to meet?"

"And today, if possible. That would be good."

"Okay, do you know where the house is? I live in Piraeus, in Maniatika."

"Wait, let me get a pen and write down the address. Come on, tell me."

"Thrace Street,15. How will you get there?"

"In my car, Nikolas."

"Remember to ask someone. Tell them that the street is near Saint Sofia, the church. It's easy, don't worry."

"I'll find it. Is six o'clock okay?"

"It's fine! We'll wait for you. I'm glad to hear from you."

"I'm glad too, Nikolas. Come on, bye for now."

At the sound of the front doorbell, a ten-year-old boy ran to open it.

"Who are you?" he asked spontaneously. "I don't know you," he added, without taking his eyes off Dimitros, whose cheeks were red from ear to ear, from the shame he felt.

"Who is it, Andrew?" They heard a bass male voice from inside the house.

"He is a big man with a mustache. There is also a big woman with him who is holding a boy by the hand, as Mom holds me!"

"Ha ha ha! Come on, Tzanis has arrived. I am coming!"

As soon as they met, the two cousins - who had not seen each other for over twenty years - fell hard into each other's arms. As they pulled away, Nikolas, holding Tzanis tightly by the shoulders, said to him:

"Welcome. Come, come in, like it's your home."

"Chiona, my cousin, Nikolas. Nikolas, my crown, Chiona, and my child, Dimitros. My daughter will come in a few days with Sabatis; do you remember him?"

"Yes, what is this seadog doing?"

"He's fine. Finally, he became a sailor; he boarded."

"Come, sit down and talk, you've met my only child. My wife will be back soon, she's gone to a neighbor."

A bright ground-floor house, with a courtyard at the back full of pots of geraniums.

The air of Mani was carried by old black-and-white photographs that decorated the living room. Cleanliness and care everywhere, everything smelled of musk; Nikolas's wife, Maria, was a real sweetheart.

As soon as she returned, she found them sitting at the living room table. She cast a warm glance at everyone. Before Nikolas could introduce them, she spoke:

"You must be Tzanis. I've heard so much about you that I feel like I know you well." And she held out her hand.

"I don't know you, nor does Nikolas; so you must be Chiona, right?" She reached out her arms and hugged her.

As soon as he let go of her, it was Dimitros' turn.

"Who are you? Will you tell me?" she asked him.

"I am Dimitros, ma'am," he replied, lowering his eyes.

"You are very shy for a boy," she told him with a smile. "It's no use being shy; when you are shy, you don't think clearly and do things you don't want to. Come, take Andrew, and play in his room. He has toys and books there. When I set the table, I will call you to eat."

"Let's go, Dimitros, come, let's go, I tell you," little Andrew shouted happily.

He looked almost pleadingly at Chiona.

"Do you mind if I sit here with you, mother? I won't bother you at all," he told her. He didn't want to be isolated with a younger child in an unfamiliar environment. The games had ended prematurely for Dimitros. With every movement he made, the fear of Tzanis hung over him. He preferred to be near his mother; her presence provided him with the security he sought.

"Yes, sit with us," she replied, once again preempting Tzanis, who was ready to burst out on him again.

"Excuse me, Andrew, can we play next time we meet? I'm a little tired today, okay?"

So, the little boy left alone and with his head bowed for his room, without Dimitros' accompaniment.

Maria set the table with a mountain of snacks. They ate and drank until they nearly burst, as they say. They laughed their hearts out, reminiscing about childhood exploits. They had so much to say that they lost track of time.

During a break, Tzanis blurted out the purpose of the visit to his cousin:

"Nikolas, please, can you take my child to your work? He missed the school year for nothing; at least until we decide what to do. He's a good and willing child."

Dimitros couldn't believe his ears. He didn't know the intentions and purpose of the visit. Could it have never crossed his father's hollow head that Nikolas might have heard some comments about him? In Mani, everything is conveyed in the air, before the mouths have time to speak. He was angry at his hypocrisy. He felt like shouting, running away, hiding. He was ashamed. He knew that Tzanis was trying to get rid of him; he didn't want him getting tangled up in his feet; he wanted to be able to blame him for everything. But, once again, he was content to lower his head, to remain silent.

A sign of the times has always been the denial of responsibility. Few were the ones who shouldered it for their mistakes. It was always someone else who was to blame for everything.

Nikolas finally agreed to let Dimitros work with him at the photo studio for a few days a week, at least for a start, then they would decide.

On their way back, about halfway through the journey, Tzanis, looking at him sideways through the car mirror, blurted out, ironically, with a haughty tone:

"Be careful, don't embarrass me again with your antics. Get your act together while there's still time. Do you hear?"

"Stop, my lord, everything will be fine; you'll see," Chiona intervened once again.

"I heard, father. Everything will change here, rest assured."

Tzanis smiled bitterly. But Dimitros smiled too - with a smile completely different from his father's.

CHAPTER TWO

A DIVINE LOVE

The Photo Studio

Dimitros hurriedly and with his head bowed, walked down Fokionos Negri, his hands deeply buried in the pockets of his coat.

The old cobblestones were dangerously slippery. The dry wind blowing had frozen even the last drop of moisture left on the worn-out paving slabs. In a corner, a brown-haired man with worn-out knitted gloves was trying to warm himself, having almost hugged his brazier. But in vain he struggled to warm his blood; a useless effort.

There were only a few passersby around, wrapped up like onions in coats and caps, but they, too, were shivering from the cold. The frost shamelessly bore witness to the teeth of January; Dimitros had never been so cold in his life. He walked quickly, carelessly, and almost fell twice. He was in a hurry; he could barely catch the metro that passed through Victoria Square at half past eight. Otherwise, he would have to wait standing for at least another half hour for the next one, or walk to Thiseio.

A little earlier, Anna had almost forcefully wrapped a dark red scarf with fringes around his neck, which matched his ruddy cheeks.

He was bothered by the rough contact of the fabric on his skin, but he never resisted Anna's care. He discussed everything with her; age, in love, is a useless detail.

On cold winter nights, they slept in each other's arms,

snuggled up, in the same bed. Her childish innocence became a sweet remedy for his grief. Anna, in Athens, was in the second year of high school, and all the teachers had nothing but good things to say about her behavior. A bright child, she adapted quickly, made friends, made girlfriends; she was doing well.

Nikolas usually grumbled when Dimitros was late.

"Let me see when you'll be on time," he would tell him, shaking his head.

In the last year, if one excludes the first months of autumn in high school, he had been enjoying his leisure time; he was always dawdling absent-mindedly and was late.

Last September, he was enrolled, without his objection, in a local night school nearby. Essentially, he chose it because he didn't want to leave his job in the photo studio. He was fascinated by the glass of the lens; through it, he could bring his dreams to life.

The way out that he was desperately seeking, away from the outcry that he was constantly experiencing, he found in the lens. As if there was an invisible genie there that transformed whatever Dimitros asked of him. His imagination galloped uncontrollably. There, he felt like a migratory bird, never staying in one homeland!

It was only him. He defined the color, the light, and the continuity.

Everything would have been better if the choice of night school had turned out positively. But this one didn't work out. His secret identity was revealed, and a new Golgotha began for him. You see, the feminine soul inside him was shamelessly betrayed by the feminine move, which did not suit it to hide in the dry male body as if he were in a hurry to show the difference between himself and the other males. And the mockery began. The class became a tasteless theater; they threw shuttlecocks at him, they put obscene little things on his desk, the cosmetic adjectives followed each other nonstop. During breaks, he was forced to stay in class. For the toilet? He didn't even think about it; he didn't even approach it from a distance. Fear reigned worse than ever in his soul. A fear that had taken root in him and made his heart bleed incessantly. Only one girl sympathized with him, Aspasia. A few times, she sat with him, wanting to help him. She insisted that they fight the outcry together; she thought that together they could. In the end, her presence next to him came out against her. They were shouting at them both until she was forced to move away from him, unable to bear it.

The pretended balance was being disrupted by anything that didn't fit into everyone's visual image at the time. You see, everyone was tidying up the boxes that housed their "incorruptible" selves, indifferent to whatever was trying to survive around them.

Every night, he would gather at home like a beaten dog, mentally crushed. Until one night, three months later, he couldn't take it anymore, he burst out in anger. He stood up his thin body, declaring to everyone that he would never set foot there again. He told them that he would become a photographer; that was all he liked. Of course, he didn't avoid the Homeric battle. Tzanis was furious; he shouted, threatened gods and demons, cursed, and hit him once again. Logically, the surrounding blocks and their surroundings must have heard him. Chiona agreed with her son's decision, and so did Anna. Finally, after a long time - unable to do otherwise in the face of Dimitros' irrevocable decision - Tzanis retreated.

Now, he was coming and going to the photo studio alone. At first, Tzanis willingly acted as a taxi driver, not because he had a good heart; he didn't. He was overshadowed by the bad things, the antics, which changed places and were now chasing him in Athens. When he was sure of the matter, as he thought, he would find various cheap excuses to avoid the routes. Sometimes the distance was his fault, sometimes the gas was expensive, sometimes the jobs that awaited him. Total bullshit, he got tired of going to Thissio, and he would spend the whole day at Hayden's Street café, drinking cheap tsipouro and playing cards with his fellow villagers. When Chiona sometimes complained about his absence, she would hit a wall.

"It's your fault," he would tell her. "Better if you came to Athens alone with your son. I was fine in Mani. Is it my fault that he's a fagot? It is your fault that you did him all the favors. Now you ask for the change? We left, and everything was ruined there."

But time knows how to cover up memories. The months passed, and little by little, everything found the rhythm that was predetermined by the universe without their knowledge. Athens was an enlightened wandering sorceress who was driving Dimitros crazy.

Every evening after work, with a well-worn Polaroid that Nikolas had given him hanging around his neck, he would happily wander the narrow alleys of Plaka, in the shadow of the Acropolis, offering smiles and souvenir photos to locals and tourists.

"Mister, Miss, photo please; thank you! Two drachmas, please!"

Most people nodded in agreement, but as soon as he took the little money they gave him, even the hairs on his head would turn red with shame.

"Thank you, sir! Thank you!" he would say, bowing slightly.

Two or three words of English were enough to make him soar through the clouds.

He thought it was something significant to be part of a dream imprinted on glossy paper that would travel the world. A thousand words all harmoniously gathered in one image. He imagined that they would surely look at such a beautiful photograph one day, mentally rewarding that dark-haired boy who had appeared unexpectedly before them like a comet, to capture, in the colors of joy, a happy moment of their lives.

But, the very next moment, he was angry with himself for allowing some to trample him, like straw on a threshing floor. And the sadness was reborn in his melancholy eyes, which immediately filled with tears. So many repressed others who forced him to pay a price for something he had not caused. All he asked for - by right - was his share of the dream. He wanted to fill his lungs, polluted by the mud thrown at him, with pure oxygen, to honestly claim what life owed him, to obtain what he truly deserved.

Was it now so important to everyone that his soul inhabited the wrong body?

He loved Nikolas very much; everything he lacked from his father, he had found in him. And Nikolas looked after him as if he were his own child. He quickly understood the hidden secrets that troubled Dimitros' soul.

He never tried to change anything about Dimitros; he accepted his truth, treating him as a person and not as a blighter who would contaminate everything around him. He had him with him everywhere. Wherever there was a wedding and a baptism, Dimitros would always hold lamps and carry cameras. In the photo studio, when he was away on outside business, Dimitros did the hard work. Do you want appointments with clients? Do you like photo deliveries with their negatives? Give and take the finances? He managed everything just fine! Some afternoons, when he wasn't going up to the Kypseli, a truckle bed in the studio would make the situation more manageable.

The First Love

One magical April night, as it turned out, everything changed.

It was that one moment when your heart starts beating like crazy, so hard that you think it will jump out of your flesh. An unexpected call to the door of the soul, which opened wide to wash away the darkness. It always happens like this, good things come when you least expect them.

Careless as he was, he tripped on a wide landing outside a small tavern in Plaka and collapsed to the ground. Passers-by gathered around him to ask him if he was okay. The poor man felt so ashamed that he could only shake his head. Suddenly, two strong hands grabbed him tightly by the armpits and lifted him into the air like a feather. Then, the same hands made him sit carefully on a wicker chair at a small iron table in the old courtyard. Confused, Dimitros looked up to see his savior. That was enough! When their gazes met, time froze. They looked each other deeply in the eyes, without having the strength to look away. They definitely knew each other, maybe not in this life, but in another, more distant one, as if they were united by an eternal, unbreakable commitment, which was impossible for them to explain.

Like Twin Flames*, who, when lost, patiently wait for each other thousands of lifetimes to meet again.

"Are you in pain somewhere?"

"No, no, I'm fine, Dimitros stammered, without stopping to look at him.

"I'm Alexander, and I'm probably the one responsible for you falling. Sorry!"

"You? No, I was careless. But what do you mean by saying you were the one responsible?"

"Well, I've been looking at you for a long time, admiring you; I probably have an evil eye. Tell me, though, I think we know each other from somewhere. Am I wrong?"

"I have the same impression, I don't know what to say!"

"I'm finishing my shift in half an hour. Do you want to wait for me to talk?"

"Yes, Alexander, I will gladly do it," replied Dimitros, with his face shining like a firefly in an enchanted forest.

*Twin Flame: The twin flame is considered our "other half soul," a soul split into two pieces that incarnated in different individuals. Some people say that meeting the twin flame is not only divinatory but also helps with spiritual awakening and self-knowledge.

Alexander was a well-built young man, two or three years older than Dimitros, with a stocky body and two eyes that resembled a bright sky.

A little later, they were walking side by side, talking calmly. They passed through almost all the alleys of Plaka to end up on the other side of the Acropolis.

The hill of Philopappos was there, waiting to hide them from looks full of hypocrisy and disgust for what made them feel happy. A forgotten rock hospitably welcomed their bodies, letting them rest on it.

The moon above the Parthenon bore witness, without being ashamed, to their unconfessed innermost feelings. How much they needed each other.

"Do you allow me, Dimitros, to hug you?"

"I said, Alexander, that you would never ask for it!"

At their first kiss, the gates of heaven opened wide and dripped honey into the souls of these creatures, who begged for this moment never to end.

From their fateful meeting onward, everything moved quickly; one moment followed another at the speed of light, as if they feared time would run out. They understood without speaking; they evolved next to each other. Without the slightest difficulty, they became one; they lived it together. For the first time in their lives, both felt this way. A dominant, intoxicated, tamer love was born that came to teach them the unspeakable things of their souls. Two male bodies surrendered to a passion that was mercilessly pursued by the public outcry. Nothing frightened them, except time, which made them suffer when they were far from each other.

They discussed living together, but, unfortunately,

some obstacles made it difficult to sail towards their dream.

Alexander, at twenty, had no particular problem. The offspring of a large, low-income family, he would not be a burden to anyone. Just the same, one less mouth. Dimitros, on the other hand, how could he blurt it out? What could he tell his family? At seventeen, how could he live with his friend? Who would dare to take him out alive from Tzanis' wrath?

The only ones who knew about this relationship were Nikolas and Anna; he trusted no one else.

In August of the following year, Nikolas decided to close the photo studio for a few days and go on vacation with his family. Dimitros begged him to lie to his family that he would go with them. He and Alexander would go somewhere else, alone. He suggested that he come and pick him up from Kypseli for the smoke and mirrors.

On the way back, in the same way, he would drop him off at his house: that way, no harm, no foul.

Nikolas' love for Dimitros won out. After thinking it over for a while, he agreed on the condition that he would be cautious. For no reason, he did not want to expose himself to his cousin's eyes. Besides, Tzanis' thuggery was well-known, and not even a God could have predicted what would happen if all this conspiracy reached his ears.

Everything went exactly as they had planned—Nikolas with his family in Parga, and Alexander with Dimitros in Paros.

But when a man makes plans, God laughs. A friend of Tzanis from the café was also vacationing in Paros. Of course, he remembered Dimitros well. He had gone to the café many times to leave his father the house keys.

In fact, he recognized him immediately. The sweet moment when he walked arm in arm with Alexander, exchanging a stolen kiss in a narrow alley of Parikia, turned into a bad time a little later.

The Nightmare

You can go blind if you see all days as the same. Every day is different, every day brings its own miracle. Be brave, take risks, there is no substitute for experience.

Alexander looked at Dimitros, smiling, with shining eyes. "Do you see what the painting on the wall says? Someone wrote it for you."

"Come on, don't bother me. If you want to know, I read it today, as soon as we entered; the writings on the painting are so true that they urge you to put them into practice. I hadn't noticed it so many times since we've been here!"

"It didn't exist, that's why you hadn't noticed it, you silly. Someone wrote it in chalk, probably recently, so that we could read it. It leaves something in some people, only indifference in others. But ask yourself, how many life lessons - maybe even pain - must this man have learned, so that he decided to share it with all of us?"

He gently pinched Dimitros' nose with the fingertips of his left hand and, abruptly, with his right, pulled him next to him.

"Come, let me hug you. I've been wanting to see you since last night."

"I missed you too, today more than ever. I couldn't wait to come and see you. I have an unspeakable fear,

Alexander. I'm afraid something bad will happen."

"Why do you say that? Is there something disturbing my spring chicken?"

"A dream disturbed me, and I've been restless since the moment I woke up."

"Do you want to tell me? Here is the good dream interpreter! Tell me, and since I see you grinning, I inform you that my grandmother -God rest her soul- taught me to explain them fluently.

The two small dimples on Dimitros' cheeks, as he smiled, smiled with him. An alloy of childish innocence with thousands of question marks on his face, trying to guess the truth or the joke!

He perched on Alexander's lap, holding his hands tightly in his. There, on the old fabric sofa of the small cafe on Mayer Street, he let his gaze wander casually for a moment at the vintage decoration. Then, he gently leaned his back on the sofa and reverently leaned his head on his beloved's shoulder.

"I was... on the seashore next to the pier of Gerolimenas, gazing at the sea. You were traveling in a small boat. I thought that if I called you out loud, my voice would travel through the air, you would hear me, and you would come. I went there every day. One day, however, I saw your ship coming. And I saw you, you were standing at the bow, like a giant gazing at the sea. How beautiful you were, my God! I started calling your name louder than ever. You saw me, yes, yes, you saw me; you raised your hand, you greeted me, and called my name. I swear to you, I heard it. I said to myself, "I will climb a rock to see it better." I started climbing, but I slipped and fell hard onto the rocks. Then everything turned red with my blood, my mouth, the sea, the stones, I tell you, everything! My strong teeth broke, and I was writhing in pain. And you didn't come to save me, you looked at me from afar, you didn't move from your place. Not even the boat was moving anymore; it had stopped, and it wasn't coming towards me. I was calling to you, but my voice was lost in the waves. I was crying, but the wind crushed my tears. Suddenly, night fell, and you slowly disappeared into the darkness with it."

Alexander understood that Dimitros' dream was sorrowful, but he didn't want to make him sad anymore.

"Calm down, my Dimitros, the dream that was meant to break your heart! It's nonsense. Here, you can exchange a few words with your father, that's all. Blood means that whatever happens will happen soon, so don't make fun of it. You'll see how right I am. But now that I've explained it to you, smile at me."

Dimitros smiled, exhaling, to drive away the worry that was squeezing his heart like an iron vice.

Alexander did not tell him how bad his dream was. He did not tell him that the death of one of his own would soon be on the threshold of his life.

Nor did he himself ever imagine the dramatic consequences that would mark Dimitros, as long as breath remained in his body.

The First Murder

At a round table, decorated with green felt on top, in the café on Hayden Street, three fellow Mani residents and a Cretan were indifferently wasting their time playing cards. The cards "accompanied" the unaccompanied tsipouro among the four, Tzanis. Imitating the others, he also cursed the luck that his gender did not suit him. The Cretan, Manolis, by name, without raising his head from the deck of cards, asks Tzanis:

"Hey Tzanis, what is your son, Dimitros, doing?"

"Why did you miss him?" He replied maliciously.

"No, really, but I haven't seen him since the summer I saw him in Paros, and I was surprised."

"When did you see my son in Paros? He's never been there. Are you, hey, and you're wrong?"

"What are you telling me now? Do I not know your son? Day after day, he didn't come here, shaking his body, and brought you the keys? He was hugging a friend of his and probably "loved" him a lot. Ask him himself; let's see what he says. My eyes never deceive me."

"You, talkative, hope you have seen well, because if you make a mistake, you are so dead. I'll find out, hey, and we'll talk again."

He got up from the table, kicking everything in his way, foaming at the mouth.

A few steps down from the café was his house. He opened the front door and closed it so hard that Chiona jumped like a goat from her terror.

"Where is your boy?" He asked her sternly.

"It's afternoon, my Tzanis, he's still at work. What happened to you that you're shaking like a fish out of water? You almost broke the door."

"Your son wasn't with Nikolas in August."

"What are you saying, we wouldn't know? Would your cousin lie to us?"

"Listen to what I'm telling you. He was in Paros with a boyfriend. I'll kill them; they won't escape. Woe to them, if it's true."

"Where did you find out?"

"Manolis saw them fooling around in Parikia. He was on vacation with his wife and daughters. The fagot made me ridiculous again."

"Don't get angry, it's a lie. My Dimitros would never do that."

"I'll go pick him up in the evening to have a little talk."

"I'll come with you too, for company, my lord."

"You sit in your kitchen, do you hear? I will go alone."

No one noticed him; he remained huddled in a dark corner of his old Opel. He set up a death trap, like a murderous viper patiently waiting for its victim. At first, he saw Alexander enter the photo studio alone. After a few minutes, he saw him again going out with Dimitros.

As soon as they came out, Alexander leaned down tenderly and kissed him on the lips. He could not have imagined that this kiss would be his last.

Anger disguised itself as death and took the form of Tzanis, who was right behind him, without anyone having time to see him. The deadly blade flashed for a moment in the murderer's hand. A bright reflection that quickly disappeared, as soon as it was stuck deep into Alexander's flesh. His rage to kill him was not stopped by the sight of innocent blood flowing like a river on the dirty sidewalk, nor by the inarticulate cries of despair of Dimitros, nor by the hands of a passerby who tried to stop him at the risk of Tzanis turning on him.

He, blinded by hatred and with unstoppable rage, continued to stab the lifeless body again and again.

Dimitros remained curled up on the ground like a wounded savage, trapped by the fear of death, powerless to intervene. A waterfall of tears continuously flooded his face. He covered his eyes with the palms of his hands; he could not see his father killing what he had loved more than his own life. He begged passersby for help, but in vain.

"Why, father? Why?" He cried at one point, tearing himself apart inconsolably.

"You'll understand why, you cuckold's asshole, now that you're going to find your boyfriend where I sent him; now you'll see why too."

A mixture of animal madness and an outburst of anger in the form of a human beast, he left his mangled victim frozen on the sidewalk, and with a look that dripped blood, he turned to Dimitros.

A loud phrase of despair was heard from the mouth of Nikolas, who had just left his shop, full of guilt for being late in understanding what had happened.

"Stay away from Dimitros!"

"You knew it, you bastard, and you keep it quiet, right? Your turn will come soon, you filthy one," Tzanis shouted at him furiously.

He didn't have time to get close to Dimitros. Nikolas fell on him and immobilized his hand that was holding the sharp blade, before cutting the thread of Dimitros' life with it.

The fight was brutal, savage! Of those who had gathered around and watched in horror, no one dared to step in to separate them. They watched helplessly, in anguish, from afar, the fight, shouting:

"Help, they are being killed."

Fortunately, someone calmer, at the beginning of the fight, went to the nearby corner kiosk and notified the police. Finally, the patrol car's siren was heard, coming furiously. Its arrival gave Nikolas a redemptive ending, but a tragic one to Tzanis. In his attempt to escape arrest, a careless step was fatal. Heavy as he was, he slipped and fell clumsily to the ground. Falling, he mortally injured his neck on the corner of the sidewalk. Death was instantaneous. It seems that the police were somewhere nearby, along with the Divine Judgment, returning the price of his deed.

Within half an hour, three ambulances were leaving the bloody corner, sirens wailing. One was carrying the dead body of Alexander, the other the lifeless body of Tzanis, and the third was carrying Dimitros, who had been thrown into a coma by the powerful shock.

A patrol car took Nikolas away in handcuffs, while a municipal crew was trying to clear the remains of a twenty-year-old life from the sidewalk.

At The Hospital

It had already been ten days since Dimitros had been hospitalized.

For the first four, in the intensive care unit, he was in a coma. On the fifth day, with the care of the doctors, he came back to life. Anna, an impenetrable rock at his side, did not even go to her father's funeral, so that she could remain by the side of her beloved brother.

Tzanis was buried in the First Cemetery of Athens despite his wish to be buried in the Holy Land, as he said, in Mani. Only a few were present whose peace of mind was not disturbed by his act. The unfortunate Chiona was trying to cope with everything alone; she again took on the burden. On the one hand, Dimitros is in the hospital; on the other, the burial, the final straw, the interrogations accompanied by shame like a black frost covering her soul.

The police were looking for the cause of the crime.

What could she tell them? Did the father kill his son's boyfriend? Even the stones would be ashamed. Finally, she was forced to say to them the whole truth, expecting that the tones that had upset their lives would drop.

Mother and daughter agreed, in Dimitros' absence, that the best thing for everyone would be to move as far away as possible, to another area, so that no one would know them. Nikolas was released the day after the incident. Several witnesses strongly supported his innocence.

When Dimitros came to in the hospital, he realized the drama of his life. He tried, fortunately without success, to commit suicide by cutting the veins in his left hand with a piece of glass from the tumbler on the bedside table next to him, which he had previously broken.

A nurse, who came in to change his serum, caught the worst. He attempted as soon as Anna left, when she went to her house to wash, eat, and change clothes. This gave him the opportunity he was looking for. He felt like a living dead with the death of Alexander. He felt an immense void in his soul. As for his murderer? Indescribable hatred. It didn't matter to him that he was his own father. After all, he had hated him for years for the psychophysical violence he had received from him.

Nikolas visited him often in the hospital, but the courage he tried to give him did not bring him comfort. He only sought the presence of Anna and his mother, no one else. When they enthusiastically told him about their plan to move to another area, he did not object. He only told them expressionlessly:

"Decide whatever you want, I am not interested."

As time passed, the grief over the loss of Alexander, instead of subsiding, raged silently within him. His tears dried up. He held wings of happiness in his hands, and before he could fly with them, his father himself cut them off.

After fifteen nightmarish days in hospital, he finally returned home. At the end of the fourth month of confinement, he secretly left home one afternoon, without anyone noticing. He wanted to pay off a debt; it was the only one left unpaid. He set out to find his father's grave. He had discreetly taken care to get some information from Anna that would lead him to the place where he was buried. He had no difficulty finding him at all. When he saw it, he stood up on the marble, spat on it, and peed on his photo.

Then he muttered, clearly satisfied:

You got what you merited, you billy goat. And you deserve it.

In Mani, when the murder was learned, there was a great commotion. Most people justified the murderer and cursed Dimitros and his mother. The few who knew him better exclaimed with joy: "He got, received one's just deserts, the wretch," they said.

CHAPTER THREE

THE FALSE STEP

Keratsini

In the summer of the fifth year after their relocation to Athens, Chiona, now seventeen-year-old Anna, and with the help of Maria, Nikolas's wife, found a three-room apartment on the second floor in Keratsini, near Maniatika. They reached an agreement with the broker who mediated, and they exchanged it for the ground floor in Kypseli. Nikolas made sure to cover a slight financial difference that arose. Two years after the murder of Alexander and the death of Tzanis, the only family that had supported them entirely and with excessive sympathy was Nikolas'—no one else.

Dimitros now lived permanently with his mother and sister in the apartment in Keratsini. A forced change that, fortunately, helped a little.

And this is because the residents there, in the refugee neighborhoods of Piraeus, were made of a different material than those in the center of Athens: uprooted people, the Asia Minor.

In the fierce barbarity they suffered, they were forced to abandon their homeland, having only pain and heartbreak as their allies. They lost everything at once, in one tragic night. Beloved ones, living beings, blossoming lives, everything turned to ashes. Everything turned into a deafening sadness, into a sad memory.

There, then, in the poor neighborhoods, life was not impersonal like in Kypseli.

You could count the apartment buildings on the fingers of one hand; the houses still had yards. Jasmines and evening primroses climbed whitewashed fences, their white flowers fragrant. Heavenly colors of carnations. Roses and geraniums saturated the gaze with sweetness. Imagine there were still dirt roads full of children playing with happy voices that filled your soul with carefreeness and happiness.

A partition wall in the three-story apartment building where they lived housed an elderly couple, Mr. Thanasis and his wife, Penelope. You could read the pain in the lines on their faces. They had lost their two children in the persecution; they did not have time to save them, and they drowned when they were thrown into the sea. Not even their lifeless bodies managed to gather; they remained there to keep company in their lost dreams. But when they saw Dimitros, they smiled. They always had something nice to say to him, to praise him.

Dimitros went back and forth with Nikolas to the photo studio every day. He silently carried his heavy cross, willfully ignoring everything that was happening in the world he was brought to live in. His eyes were constantly watery, sunk deep in despair with no end. He lived without getting over the loss of his beloved. He did not eat or speak; you could barely get words out of his mouth. He constantly cursed the mistake of nature that only caused him pain.

Nothing interested him anymore, not even those evenings that he loved so much, when the camera lens embraced his imagination, so that they could travel together through the narrow alleys of Plaka. For him, there was only an empty, cold, distant world; an absolute void. Alexander's smiling face was permanently etched in his mind, and his ears were still tingling from the beautiful words he had heard from him: "I will always love you." Remember that, my little one. Always. What a deceptive word; its life lasts only a few moments, then it loses its essence.

Each day, a miserable imprint identical to the previous one, as if someone were using the same old stamp with a well-worn pad.

And the hours, the days, the months passed, without time becoming omni-taming this time. When hope loses its light, darkness drowns it.

At the cost of his soul, Dimitros was forced to pay the price of social condemnation for his love anarchy.

He constantly tasted the depreciation, which, like a poison, slowly flowed through his blood.

An enslaved bird's heart, fluttering ceaselessly, terrified, within the rusty cage of public opinion.

The sweet taste of Alexander's love and affection had been lost forever, and in the worst way. Trapped in his Gordian Knot, he accepted, without reaction, the sealed check bearing his name.

He fought with all his remaining strength to hide what was no longer hidden.

Nature had done her job well. The feminine identity was now gushing out so openly that it made the male body ashamed.

Permanently locked up at home, he looked naked in the mirror and was angry at the creator's mistake. He hated the body that carried his soul.

There were times when he was forced to go, reluctantly, with Nikolas for a wedding photo shoot. He envied the couple's happiness; his insides were sticking out, and he was in unbearable pain. He knew that this ceremony for him was an unattainable dream.

Dimitros, with Anna and Chiona, usually sat on the second-floor north balcony on spring afternoons. From there, when the sun began to set, they would gaze at Mount Egaleo, which cast its imposing shadow over them. The treeless, rocky mountain bore witness to images and memories of the Mani they had abandoned.

Chiona had taken a job at a small traditional bakery in Piraeus. Every morning, she would leave at dawn, like a thief. This happened every day; she would rest on one Sunday, and not always.

When her brother, Sampatis, disembarked, he went to find them. When Chiona found her brother, she asked him to sell their entire belongings in Mani on her behalf. The olive trees, the olive press, the house, the barren fields, everything. She never wanted to see Mani again. None of them wanted to. She had something secretly etched in her mind to do for Dimitros, but for now, she kept it a closely guarded secret. Sampatis, carrying out her strict orders to the letter, managed to sell most of their property in Mani. A few worthless acres of barren land remained on some uncharted mountain ridges; they left these to their fate. The Maniot mother deposited the money in the bank. When asked what she planned to do with it, she would bluntly reply that the money had a sacred purpose. Only she knew.

Meeting Christos

One Saturday night, after months of confinement, Dimitros felt like he was suffocating. A knot of despair was gnawing at his throat, robbing him of his breath.

He was desperately asking for oxygen; he went out onto the apartment balcony in search of fresh air. Anna was away, and Chiona was cooking in the kitchen. Hearing the violent creak of the balcony door as it opened, she shouted:

"My Dimitros, are you okay?"

She repeated her son's name a couple more times. There was no answer.

Frightened, she went to the living room. Dimitros was not there.

The balcony door was wide open, with the white curtains blowing in the spring breeze.

"Dimitros, my Dimitros," she called again.

"Here I am, mother, don't shout," he said in a low voice.

"You scared me, my boy."

"This 'my boy'... can you finally stop it, please?"

And, tightly gripping the railing he was holding, he continued with a clear sob:

"What were you afraid of, mother, that I shouldn't fall? I went out to get some air. I was suffocating in the four walls. Besides, what are you worried about? I've been dead for a long time now."

"Don't say things like that now, everything will pass. Go out for a while, and your mood will change."

"And where should I go? Wherever I go, they shout at me. I'm tired of it."

"Don't pay attention, Dimitros, to what you hear. What matters is what you think of yourself, not what others say."

He stared at her intently. Sighing, he let his gaze travel to her eyes. He let go of the railing he was holding, lovingly nestling his hands in hers.

"As if you're right, mommy, I'm going out. If my Anna were here, I'd take her with me; she'd know where to go."

Without wasting any more time, he quickly put on a loose white shirt and tight jeans, put on a pair of white shoes, and opened the front door to leave. As he left, he heard Chiona say to him:

"My dear, don't be sad. I will always be here for you."

"Thank you, mother," he replied, closing the door softly.

Sometimes he would think about going to Piraeus. He wanted to go back to Pasalimani, but the postponements kept coming. Once in his life, quite some time ago, on a sunny Sunday morning, he went with his beloved. They had walked together all along the Marina of Zea, and they reached the lighthouse. There, Alexander had embraced him and had promised him that he would never abandon him. How could the unfortunate man have known the writings of his fate?

Arriving at the square, he stood at the bus stop. He looked right, then left, hoping to find someone to tell him which bus to take. An old lady standing a few meters away, with a glance, guessed his intentions.

"Can I help you with something, my young man?"

"You know, I'm new to the area," Dimitros replied, bowing his head shyly. "I don't know which bus to take to go to Piraeus."

"I didn't know either when I first arrived," she told him, smiling. "It's simple, it says it on the 'forehead'. You'll see it as soon as it arrives. I'm waiting for that too."

"Thank you very much," he said, returning the smile.

Not even ten minutes had passed when he was boarding the old vehicle. It took him another ten to reach Ippodamia Square.

Two young men passing by whispered something lewd to him as he disembarked, but he paid no attention. The port and the streets were brightly lit. A soft breeze with a salty taste pierced his nostrils. Some groups, mainly of young people, crowded here and there. They were cheerfully organizing the program they would follow. Saturday night is a classic evening of entertainment.

His loneliness, an unseen fellow passenger, fell like a dark sheet, flattening his soul. Quickly wiping away the uninvited tears that rolled down his cheeks, he cursed his father angrily, once again.

Fifty meters below, there was a kiosk, illuminated by multicolored lamps and filled with excess goods. From a distance, it reminded you of a small illuminated mail boat traveling on land.

"A pack of tissues, please," he asked the kiosk attendant, who was looking at him provocatively, like almost everyone else.

"Fifty cents," he replied, giving Dimitros what he asked for.

"Thank you very much. Can I ask you a question?"

"If I can help you, why not?" the kiosk attendant replied.

"How can I get to Pasalimani?"

"The answer is easy! You will go straight, pass the church, and reach the town hall square. At the end of it, turn right, then left at the first one. It will take you where you want to go. Do you understand?"

"Yes, yes! I understand, thank you!"

"Whatever you want, babe. At your disposal," the kiosk man replied slyly.

Dimitros lowered his head and left, without saying a word.

Arriving at the Holy Trinity church, he crossed to the opposite sidewalk, took a deep breath, and continued. Now and then, he stopped to stare in ecstasy at the large shop windows on Vasileos Georgiou Street. Walking, he crossed perpendicularly what is now Iroon Polytechniou Street, after the brightly lit square that was full of people. Finally, he turned right onto Sotiros Street, which reached as far as Pasalimani. His heart skipped a beat at the sight of the windows filled with women's clothes, shoes, and jewelry. He imagined himself in them, and a wave of bliss flooded him.

He could no longer resist the call of nature. He felt like a woman; it was his truth, and as a woman, she wanted to enjoy what rightfully belonged to her. These thoughts gave him the strength to accept, to move forward, and to take back what society's stereotypes had deprived him of. Unfortunately, this strength weakened in the immediate moments in front of the mockery and contempt he received from most of the men who approached him.

The old clock in Pasalimani showed half past nine. He crossed the road and sat on the first step of the main entrance to the marina. Couples, groups of friends, and some loners were making a soulatso back and forth - a pure bride market. He, with sadness, looked at the luxurious yachts gently rocking and touching one another. He dreamed of getting into one of them, of getting lost, of leaving, of never coming back. Then he regretted it; at least here, he monologued to himself, he had his mother, he had Anna, he knew they loved him and would stand by him no matter what. Abandoned in the armada of his thoughts, he did not realize when a young man discreetly sat down next to him.

"Am I bothering you?" he asked in a low voice.

Dimitros' heart skipped a beat at the stranger's sudden presence.

He turned, frightened, towards the newcomer, to answer:

"You scared me, omg! I was distracted," he told him.

"Forgive me, I didn't mean to. Well, I passed you two or three times, and when I looked at you, I realized your thoughts were wandering. Do you want some company?"

Without hearing a condescending answer, he sat down almost next to him.

A young man, older than Dimitros, extremely stocky, with long brown hair and dark eyes, whose eyes you had difficulty reading. He was wearing a short-sleeved black T-shirt with a photo of the Doors on the front, faded jeans, and dark leather boots.

"You can sit where you sat; the steps are public. As for whether I want company, it will depend..."

The stranger laughed out loud.

"My name is Christos. Yours?"

"Me, Dimitros. Do you want a surname?" He replied with a small dose of irony.

"Come on, relax. I'm lonely too. I want company."

"When you say 'company', what do you mean? What can you say to a stranger?"

"Don't label me. If I'm a burden to you, tell me to leave."

Christos's manner and expression were enough to make Dimitros' defensive shields fall a little.

"No, sit down, you're not a burden. I'm just not used to making acquaintances so easily. Forgive me if I was a little abrupt. Do you come here often?"

"Not so much. I live in Alexandroupolis. My origin is from Moldova. I came to Greece when I was very young. I work in Thessaloniki at a distribution company, and I come to Piraeus and Athens at most two or three times a month with a colleague."

"I understood from your accent that you are not Greek."

"Is this bad for you?"

"Of course not. I am the last one to judge you; as if I will marry you?" he said jokingly.

"You, where are you from?"

"Me? From Mani. I'm a native, tough Maniatian, it seems; don't you think?" Dimitros continued to joke. "Four years ago, we first came to Athens, and recently I moved to Keratsini. I'm into photography."

"Dimitros, how old are you?"

"Are you a registry office?" He replied, laughing. "How old do you think I am?"

"Nineteen!"

"You miser... put one more in, and you'll be fine. What about you, Christos?"

"I turned twenty-eight last month."

"May you become a centenarian," he replied with a bit of coquetry.

"Dimitros, my ass froze to the marble for so long. What do you say, there's a lovely cafe nearby, Fontana. Be my guest."

"Yes, let's go! Why not. And my own ass is complaining."

"I would tell you, me to warm it up, but the place is not convenient."

"Satyr, shame on you!" He replied, laughing.

The need for contact and Christos' straightforward approach were more than enough to create something that would instantly eliminate Dimitros' inhibitions.

It was obvious what he wanted; he didn't bother to hide it. Dimitros was left to his heart's content and could go wherever it pleased. But this "will" would take him too far.

A little later, at a remote coffee table, they enjoyed the coolness of their iced cocktails.

The accumulated sadness and the ignorance of alcohol led Dimitros to talk incessantly about everything that had happened in his life. When he mentioned Alexander, his eyes filled with tears. Christos listened to him carefully, without interrupting him once.

He unlocked him with key questions, forcing him to tell him everything. As soon as he finished the first one, he asked for a second drink and then a third. That's when everything around him went dark, and he passed out.

Christos raised his right hand, palm closed and index finger extended, for the waiter to see. The waiter's experienced gaze directed him to the table where they were seated. Approaching them, he easily discerned the state Dimitros was in.

"What would you like, please? Can I help with something?" He asked politely.

"Where can I call? My friend, who is not a drinker, had a little too much to drink and, apparently, he is drunk. I want to tell a mutual friend to come pick us up in his car.

"You will find a phone next to the bar. Ask the bartender to show you...

"If you need anything for your friend, ask me; don't hesitate. It's clear that the man needs help; he's really bad."

"Okay, thank you. If necessary, I'll tell you," Christos told him.

The phone was indeed next to the bar. A thick phone book sat on a square table, a phone on top of it.

With quick movements, he dialed a number on the round dial. On the third call, a bored male voice answered.

"Who is it?"

"Jimmy, it's me. Come to Fontana in your car now. I've caught a windfall. Come on, let's party, don't be late."

"Hang up, I'm coming. I'll be there in twenty minutes."

Unparalleled Violence

In exactly twenty minutes, a black Toyota sedan with tinted windows rang its alarm at the eastern edge of Pasalimani Square. A short, fair-skinned man with rugged features, about thirty, wearing a black t-shirt, stepped out of the driver's door. He paused for a moment, searching with his eyes for his friend among the few remaining patrons in the café.

Christos, however, had already noticed him. He almost picked up the fainting Dimitros and walked towards the parked car.

"Jimmy, open the back door," he called out to him as he approached.

"Where did you find him? Really drunk!" He told him, laughing, in chewed Greek, opening the back door as he spoke. Seeing Dimitros' mess, he added sarcastically:

"Should we empty him into the trunk? If he throws up, he'll make a mess of everything. I cleaned it up yesterday."

"He won't throw up; he didn't drink much. He'll recover quickly."

Falling into the back seat, Dimitros was moaning, panting, recovering for a few seconds, and then fainting again.

Next to him, Christos was gently caressing his neck, still aroused. A curl that was lying on his cheek was captivating him even more.

"Jimmy, the little guy, is really turning me on. Do you want us to fuck him together? He won't feel much, the way he is. What do you say?"

"I like it. Where do you want us to take him?"

"He's not for the house; he has a problem. If he comes to his senses and starts shouting, we'll get into trouble. Let's see how he goes first, and then we'll decide. Go to the boatyard in Haravgi, behind the PPC factory. Not a single soul there."

In less than half an hour, they parked at the end of

the dirt road that led to the small harbor. It was past two in the morning, with the crescent moon lying on its back, casting its weak, pale light on the undulating waters. A few seagulls that had been sitting on the rocks flew away, screaming at the intruders who had disturbed their peace.

"Wait, Christos, let me turn off the light from the ceiling lights so no one notices us, you never know," said Jimmy, opening the driver's door.

Christos put his hand inside Dimitros' shirt and began to caress his chest. Jimmy tried to take off his pants, and when he succeeded, he violently pulled his underwear, tearing it. A dirty desire had taken over both of them, as messy as the rocks around the spilled oil. They began to take turns raping him hard, over and over. Their repressed instincts, river-like, flowed endlessly. Dimitros had slowly started to come to his senses, but that did not deter them. As time passed, he came closer to a nightmarish reality. He was intensely resentful of the pressure of his rapists; he suffered, and he was in pain. Instinctively, in his daze, he began to call for help.

"Shut your mouth, dirty little fag, you're pretending you don't like it," whispered Jimmy, giving him a hard slap.

"Put the underwear in his mouth to shut up, Jimmy," Christos added.

They dragged him naked out of the car, and they led him to the helm of a half-broken, forgotten boat, where they tied his hands. Gagged and tied, he was unable to offer any resistance to what fate had in store for him that endless night. He accepted the torture he was experiencing, crying, begging for it to end as quickly as possible, but unfortunately, it was too early for that.

When they had satisfied their appetites, they dressed him as they could and removed the underwear from his mouth. He was half-fainting; they grabbed him by the arms and legs and squeezed him, tied and exhausted, into the trunk of the car. They entered the vehicle's cabin without starting immediately. They preferred to wait a bit in case a passerby had seen them.

When they were sure no one was watching, they started.

"Should we dump him, Christos? Or pimping him out to the sidewalk?"

"He's not for the sidewalk, didn't you see? Unless we throw him in the junk, but then again, I don't know, he's stupid, we'll only have trouble with him. Let's go and throw him up in Troumba, let them pick him up from there. We, however, had our fun."

Dimitros, on the way, came to his senses. Realizing where he was, bathed in pain and fear, he panicked even more. He then began to cry hysterically for help. He was kicking the trunk of the car like a madman, with all the strength left in his tamed soul.

Self-preservation, climaxing in despair, won out over his reactions.

Seeing his unexpected reaction, Jimmy quickly left the main road, turned sharply right, and stopped in a dark alley of Drapetsona.

"I'll tear the bastard apart before he gets us into trouble," he growled, opening the door.

"Watch out, Jimmy, we're not for that now. Scare him."

"I will scare the asshole. Don't worry!"

A cut from the sharp knife and a few strong punches

to Dimitros' face were enough to make him lose consciousness again.

The last patrons staggered awkwardly, trying to emerge one by one from the front doors of the Troumba's cabarets. Their clothes reeked of smoke and cheap perfumes. Some sang out of tune, the last song they heard, and held on wherever they could, so as not to collapse like empty sacks. Some "sentimentalists" held their market "Aphrodite" tightly in their arms, so that she would not run away. The hotelier of Lux in Filonos Street treasured such hours. As time passed, every Tom, Dick, and Harry crept out, like mice, to hide from the light of day, which would bear shameless witness to the debauchery of the night. Veteran old women, adorned like music barrels, in the role of cruel pimps, were trying to fill in hours of work, while there was still time, for their "protected" girls.

A hunchback selling bagels and a skinny peddler of salep circled like haunted bats afraid of the light. Their voices mingled with those of the thugs who threw drunk and freeloaders into the street, beating them with sticks. The lights of the bars and cabarets went out one after the other, and the signs depicting the beauties of strippers had come to an end.

At the forbidden crossroads of Troumba, a group of rookie soldiers ran in panic, hurrying to catch the morning report to the Kopi camp in Drapetsona. The daring allure offered by the striptease of a Brazilian dancer, with the paid accessories of her companionship, made them lose their marbles.

Next to the cabaret Argentine, in Filellinon Street,

almost behind the half-collapsed door of a forgotten warehouse, Dimitros' bloody shirt stood out. Two or three 'respectable' lovers of the night stopped to stare. He, bloodied, frozen, unconscious, with a knife wound that started next to his left ear and ended under his jaw. His bruised wrists revealed the sadism of anthropomorphic monsters who, to satisfy their perversion, plundered human flesh. A young lady, probably a cleaner, coming out of a bar with a bucket in her hand, noticed him and shouted:

"Help, they killed the lad! Help, someone, please!"

Two policemen on duty, hearing her, ran over. As soon as they saw the bleeding Dimitros, they bent over him. One of them, coolly, touched the carotid artery in his neck with his two fingers.

"Quickly, call an ambulance, he still has a pulse," he told his colleague. He continued, shouting angrily to the curious people, who had meanwhile made a huddle around:

"Wrap him in something. Why are you staring at him like idiots? The man is frozen."

"Give me a moment, I'll get my coat," said the kind-hearted cleaning lady.

"Does anyone know anything about this?" the constable asked pompously.

"I know something, officer," replied a half-naked escort, who had obviously not yet finished her shift. "Here, sir, I took off my miserable body at four o'clock to get some air. You see, the strays are busting my chops. While I was sucking in the oxygen, I caught sight of two scoundrels - one tall and one short - dragging the poor fellow and leaving him in the warehouse. I said nothing and gathered myself in my place. I don't mess with them. However, I was sure that something was wrong with the young man; he wasn't moving at all."

"Can you describe them?"

"Well... what can you see in the dark? Every night, the same thing happens. Anyway, it seemed like they got balls; they were both brawnies. You didn't call them saints."

"Okay, okay, stop by the department later to give a statement, did you hear? Don't you dare not come, because then I'll come find you."

"Okay, I got the hint, I'll come."

The familiar sound of the ambulance siren escorted Dimitros to the State Hospital of Nice. Unconscious, raped, and seriously injured, with the attendant rescuers struggling to keep the thread of his life alive.

Seriously Injured

Just before the sun shone brightly on the world, Chiona jumped up in fright from her sleep. A mother's instinct, full of worry, warned her that something was wrong with her child. Her heart fluttered loudly when she saw Dimitros' bed empty. The unwrinkled sheets were a clear sign that he had not slept there.

She quickly went to Anna's room. She gently put her hand on her shoulder and nudged her. She opened her eyes sleepily.

"What happened to you that you are waking me up so early on a Sunday, Mom? Did something happen?"

"Get up, Anna... Our Dimitros went out for a walk early yesterday. He hasn't come back yet; something bad has happened to him!"

"Come on, Mom. Don't worry, he'll get into trouble somewhere; he's grown up now."

"My instinct is infallible. Come on, get up, I tell you."

"Okay, okay... I'm getting up. Go inside, and I am coming."

The hours passed nightmarishly slowly. Dimitros was nowhere to be seen. Anxiety began to grip Anna as well. Chiona sat in a chair, holding her head, sobbing. At one point, Anna stood up in front of her.

"Don't cry, Mom. Put on your jacket and let's go."

"Where should we go, my daughter? Who can help us find our Dimitros?"

"To the police, Mom. Let's go ask; they might know something."

Within minutes, the officer on duty at the Keratsini police station informed them that, according to a signal they had received, a serious injury had been reported in Piraeus involving a young person of unknown identity. This person was being treated at the hospital in Nikaia. He was the only incident that matched their search; the rest concerned women and older people.

The taxi with the two women stopped at the entrance to the State Hospital.

Upset, they went to the information desk. They were talking incoherently to the employee, who tried in vain to calm them down. Finally, they reached an agreement, and the employee made two or three phone calls in their presence. That's how they found the room where Dimitros was being treated. A young doctor who was finishing his shift happened to be passing by. Hearing the incident, he stopped next to them.

"Excuse me, he told them. I happened to hear your problem. I think I saw the person you're looking for. He came by emergency ambulance this morning."

"Is he okay, doctor? Tell me, please," Chiona asked him, crying.

"Don't worry, he's fine now. He'll tell you himself when he comes to. He'll need your care and love. He must have been through some tough times. When you see him, please don't bother him. He needs some peace. Okay?"

"Thank you very much, doctor," Anna replied, shaking his hand.

Dimitros' swollen, bruised face, the gauze covering the stab wound, the bruises on his hands, and the serums slowly dripping life drop by drop into his body, all of these were tangible evidence of the night that had passed. Nothing more was needed for the two women to understand what had happened to him. Sighing, Chiona approached her unconscious son. She reverently took his hand in hers and raised her head high.

"Thank you, God, that he is alive."

Then she turned her gaze on him with affection and mumbled enigmatically.

"I promise you, my child, everything will change starting tomorrow. The time has come for everything to fall into place."

CHAPTER FOUR

THE MOMENT WHEN EVERYTHING CHANGED

The Trip To Casablanca

In the port of Piraeus, the atmosphere suffocated you with the smell of salt, spilled oil, and heavy humidity. It was dawning, and the night, defeated by the light, in decay, surrendered its scepters.

Every day is another day. There are no givens; the givens change from one moment to the next in the twinkling of an eye. As if there is a higher plan of life for everyone, which no one can avoid, but neither can they change; this is called destiny. You never escape it.

The ship Synthia was untying its ropes, ready to set sail. From its chimney, the black smoke looked like a gaunt monk dancing to the rhythm of the morning breeze. The hoarse loudspeakers were giving the last reminder to board. The seagulls, known gossipers, were screaming, taking walks above the ship as if ordering the last late passengers to hurry. At the customs checkpoint, a guard opened Dimitros' suitcase and found inside the two dresses that Chiona had bought him. He looked at him enigmatically, persistently for a moment, and then closed it without saying a word. Just one look, that one with half hesitation, half respect. A look that he would never forget.

After they finally managed to board, Dimitros, embracing the dream dressed in the costume of hope, went to the back of the deck. He held the round white railing of the stern in his palms and waited patiently to set sail to redemption. He was wearing a light green coat with slightly short sleeves. The collar was turned up to hide the gash that Jimmy had given him that night; how ashamed he was of it—six months had already passed since he came face to face with death, because he asked the wrong person, at the wrong time, for love. The pimps were finally arrested. The descriptions of the cabaret girl burned them. She knew them, and well, but fear kept her mouth shut. When the cops forced her to testify, she knew everything. Both of them were fragrant flowers; they put them in the clink for at least a decade. They quickly "got" Christos in the clink. He had open accounts with his former associates; he had nailed them to get away with it. When they met him, they set him up and stabbed him.

Dimitros' entire belongings were a small suitcase, a passport, an identity card, and dozens of bad memories that he intended to drown in the waters of the Mediterranean. Casablanca in 1973 was not only a hub of cultures, but also a refuge for people who wanted to either get lost or find themselves again. There, in this African city, on a forgotten, dusty avenue, there was a well-known, good doctor in an old clinic. There was also hope, along with the promise of a new beginning. Chiona had everything well organized. She had been thinking about it for years, without saying a word. She asked, read, searched in secret, experienced firsthand the misery of her child's life, and she wanted at all costs to put a definitive end to it. She sold whatever was for sale and worked as hard as he could, waiting for the right moment to speak.

Anna agreed without a trace of reaction, and so did

Nikolas. Dimitros was the last to find out, when he had recovered entirely from his rape.

"My child, the time has come to correct the mistake," Chiona told him. She explained to him everything that concerned him, and they would come into effect as soon as she received his consent. While she was talking, Dimitros, on his knees, kissed her hands, tears of joy streaming down his face.

"Thank you, my mother. Thank you!" he told her.

He stood on his feet and hugged her tightly for a while, telling her in a whisper:

"I would be lost without you. My God, how I love you."

Chiona was putting their clothes in the small closet of the narrow interior cabin on the second deck. From the porthole, the harbor jetty could be seen in the distance, with the lighthouse proud as a peacock. She carefully took one of her own light-colored coats, took out the rest of the clothes from the suitcase, folded them again, and put them back in their original places. In one sense, this garment was precious. On its inner lining, she had sewn a dream of keeping company with a respectable amount of money, which would be the source of their expenses. She had a deep belief about life, a rule that she made sure to convey often to her children:

"Because life goes on," she would say. "But those who claim it, live it more deeply."

The first stop on the journey is beautiful Marseille. The ship's trip would take about three days. Next to their cabin, a plump Italian nun, with a cross in her hand, was talking about the Virgin Mary and sinners. Chiona, coming out, literally fell on her. She greeted her with a nod and a smile, since she knew very well that sometimes silence is salvation.

She met Dimitros at the stern, meditating expressionlessly.

He was wearing an old gray suit. Her discreet perfume, with the smell of jasmine, mingled with the fragrance of the sea. The sunlight, golden and quiet, fell on their shoulders like a blessing. She touched him gently on the shoulder and, with a voice like a velvet caress, said to him:

"We only look ahead, my Dimitros, only ahead!"

"Yes, mother, you're right. It's just this: people's looks, I can't stand them. How much they scare me. I feel like I have a sign on me that says where I'm going and what I'm going to do. In a few days, though, they'll call me out as they should," he told her with a touch of cruelty, at the same time letting his gaze ride wildly on his imagination.

The sea around them is deep blue, deep, like their thoughts. From the ship's loudspeakers, Edith Piaf is playing softly, the air smells of salt and freedom, and for the first time, he feels that he will never regret it.

In his pocket, the tip of a letter he had written could be seen, to send when the time came, to his old self; the one he had left forever in the port of Piraeus, to keep company with the ghosts of yesterday. Because now, he was welcoming the woman who was coming inside him.

After two and a half days of quiet travel, they were approaching the south of Sardinia. They were only a few hours away from the first stop on their journey, Marseille.

From the high deck, as they approached, the old town was clearly visible. From the port, the city seemed to climb hills with stone houses and cobblestone streets full of stories that might have been forgotten, but maybe not. Marseille in 1973 was a city full of vitality, cultural diversity, and charm. They would only stay a few hours, just enough to wait for the passengers who had a stop in Marseille to disembark, and for those whose destination was Casablanca to board.

The atmosphere smelled of fish, pine, and ink. It was afternoon. Chiona held his hand and said:

"We have time to go for a short walk, do you want to?"

"Can we?"

"We can do anything, if we want to, my Dimitros. Come on, let's go, we won't be late."

She held his hand, even as they were going down the stairs. A sailor nodded to them not to be late. Chiona winked at him, saying:

"We'll be back soon, rest assured. Thank you."

Dimitros, as soon as he set foot on solid ground, stopped short.

It's the first step in a city that doesn't know me, he thought. And maybe that's the most beautiful thing, for everyone to know you for the first time, as you really are.

They walked along the main street of the city, between flower shops, bookstores, and bistros with tables overlooking the sea. Chiona bought two small croissants and gave them to him wrapped in paper.

"This is the ladies' afternoon," she said with a teasing smile. Perhaps it was her way of telling him: I see you, I accept you, I love you. Go ahead, don't be afraid.

Returning to the ship, a short stop at a chapel for a prayer with a candle in hand. Not for the change, but for peace and for a new beginning that won't hurt.

With a long whistle, the ship Cynthia slowly began to move away from Marseille, setting course for its final destination: distant Casablanca.

This line in particular had a special atmosphere, full of mystery and nostalgia. On the ship, there was a real Mediterranean polyphony. By day, the deck was filled with people: some played cards, others listened to the radio, and some read—a small community on the waves.

An older man, at one end of the deck, the wind blowing his worn trench coat, stood, leaning on the railing. He held a small leather suitcase in his hands, perhaps all that was left of his years as a worker in Marseille. He kept his gaze south, in the darkness, where he imagined the lights of Casablanca waiting for him; perhaps a woman, or a child he had not yet met. Beside him, a mother softly sang to her infant, wrapped in a blanket, to sleep.

The engines were humming, and the sound of the waves was a constant companion. From the next cabin, an older adult could be heard snoring in time with the engines.

Dimitros could not sleep. His mother, in the next bunk, was sleeping soundly. He was traveling in his own new world, which was opening its arms more and more to accept him. He knew very well that nothing would be easy.

Chiona had made sure, with the help of a family friend, a doctor, that she was informed about the entire process of change.

Change for me is not a transition. It's a return. I'm going back to where I've always been, only now the world will see it, Dimitros thought, with joy flooding every last cell in his body.

When the ship finally reached port, four days later, there on the edge of the Atlantic, it whistled loudly. The land of Morocco unfolded like a forgotten photograph, perhaps a little dusty, maybe a little blurry, but all its own.

Late in the afternoon, they disembarked. An older man in a corner of the port sold them dates from a basket. Dimitros, not knowing the dialect, contented himself with communicating through body language, bowing. He replied something in Arabic that, later, he learned meant: He who walks with truth never gets lost.

They arrived in Casablanca very tired. Dimitros had lost some weight, but with every step he took, it seemed that something had changed radically inside him. Something had solidified, and he was no longer moving; he felt more whole than ever. They rented a small room in Medina, the old city, in a house with blue shutters.

The courtyard was full of jasmine climbing the walls and flowers fragrant all around. The owner was a plump old lady, probably a widow, Madame Bouket. Silent, serious, but with a warm look. She didn't ask questions. Every morning, she left them two cups of coffee with cardamom and some bread with honey. The first two days, they spent walking around the local market. The sun, hot, forced them to take shelter in the tents of the vendors now and then, which stretched as far as the eye could see. The sounds of the street, the horns, the voices, the music from old radios, mixed inelegantly with the smell of spices and perfumes.

The third day was scheduled for the first doctor's visit at the clinic.

The address was written on a piece of paper that had been folded and unfolded so many times that it had become almost transparent: Rue du Capitaine de frégate Jacques Lapébie. They stood for a few minutes in front of the clinic door. There was a discreet sign with the name Park and a rusty bell. Chiona pressed it hesitantly, once; then again, more forcefully. A woman with gray hair tied tightly at the back of her head opened it. Her gaze was stern, searching. Without saying a word, she stepped aside and motioned them through. They walked down a narrow corridor. The walls were painted a faded green and smelled strongly of phenol. They passed a series of closed doors. At the back was an office, behind which was the doctor. Tall, thin, with hands that reminded me of a pianist. It was Dr. Georges Burou - the man who had given life to more people than God himself had brought into the world. So the rumors went. In the visitors' chair, right in front of him, a dark-skinned man in a sariki, whose feet barely touched the floor, introduced himself in broken Greek as Apdul. He was the translator who had closed the office that Chiona had contacted when she organized the trip. After the necessary introductions were made, the doctor looked deep into Dimitros' eyes.

"It will hurt," he told him, and Abdul translated.

"I'm already in pain, doctor," he replied.

When he heard the answer from Abdul, the doctor smiled condescendingly, without adding anything. He didn't ask him why. There was no need—the why was visible in his eyes. Before the operation, the days of waiting sometimes hid an invisible fear or revealed hope—necessary rituals of the soul that enlivened a new existence.

A week later, after the necessary tests had been done, the doctor told them:

"We are ready."

The night before the operation, Chiona went out to buy something light to eat. Dimitros found the opportunity to stand naked in front of the cracked mirror of the cheap inn where they were staying. These are the unique, fragile, almost sacred moments, where the body struggles to meet the soul. He was seeing his male body for the last time. He was glad that he would never see it again. After all, he never loved it; he considered it the reason for the moil he suffered.

The clinic was quiet on the morning of the operation. The sun passed unhindered through the blinds, creating golden swords. Dimitros had slept little out of impatience. And Chiona too, but for different reasons. All alone, in a distant and unknown place for her, agonizing over the outcome of a surgical procedure that could turn into something truly shocking in Dimitros' life. You're not saying that lightly!

The nurse, a young Moroccan woman called Arzu, held his hand before the anesthesia. She said something to him in Arabic that Dimitros didn't understand, but he felt it as a wish, as a prayer. Dr. George Burou stood nearby, calm, almost ceremonial.

There was nothing distant in his presence. He knew that he was not just operating on a body; he was unlocking a soul. The anesthesia came like a wave, like white light.

And then, absolute darkness.

When he woke up, Dimitros felt nothing, not even pain. He was only aware of the weight of the blankets, the smell of the antiseptic, and the oblivion of the anesthesia slowly leaving his body. Then he heard a familiar voice. Arzu was at his headboard as if she had never left.

"Welcome back," she told him in English. He turned, looked at her, and sank back into Morpheus' arms.

The rest of the first day was a blur.

Figures came and went, the clock on the wall melted time. But inside, he felt that something had changed forever. Not abruptly, not like a transformation in a fairy tale, but quietly, deeply.

As time passed, he felt his body begin to ache. But it was his own pain, not like the one he had carried for so many years, the invisible, the mute. This one was very different. It was the pain of his redemption.

On the fourth day, with the help of Chiona, he stood for the first time in front of the mirror in the clinic room.

His body was not yet entirely his own, but it was beginning to be.

"I will call you Hope," said Chiona, clearly tearful. "That is the only name that suits you, my daughter."

Upon hearing this sentence, Hope burst into tears of joy. She now clearly understood that her ordeal was coming to an end. At least, that's what she believed.

During the days she was hospitalized, Chiona made sure to find better accommodation closer to the clinic so that Hope could, after she was discharged, take her tests and attend her doctor's appointments. The process of her complete reintegration required hormonal and psychological support as well as legal assistance, all inextricably linked with patience. Every morning, she woke up, one step closer. She now wore her new clothes without fear. She stood in front of the mirror and learned about her new face, not the one the doctor gave her, but the one that had always belonged to her. With each passing day, Hope felt less like a fugitive and more like a pilgrim.

During their stay, Chiona taught her how to tie her scarf to highlight her eyes; how to walk with her head held high without appearing provocative; how to respond when she was looked at without being embarrassed.

With A New Identity

They left Casablanca one dawn three months later, with the taste of bitter coffee and a few tears. They left behind the small clinic, Arzu, the doctor, the smell of cumin, and the soft song of the muezzin that could be heard from every crack.

On the return ship, Hope saw the horizon with clear

eyes. For the first time, she did not want to hide from anyone.

At the customs office in Piraeus, the clerk's gaze indicated that he remembered her.

The ID still had the name 'Dimitros,' but his eyes slid over her without suspicion—just a raised eyebrow. But she didn't lower her gaze: the light, the streets, the smell of gasoline in Piraeus. Everything was the same, everything familiar and distant. But she felt like a stranger. They first went to their house in Keratsini. She didn't go inside right away. She sat on the bench across from the small park, smoked a cigarette, and let her gaze wander to the second-floor balcony. When the apartment door opened, Anna, seeing them and quickly over the first shock, fell into their arms.

You see, theory is miles away from practice.

"My Anna, let me introduce your sister to you," said Chiona, jokingly.

"This is Hope," she continued, beaming with joy and happiness!

The first months were tough. The strange looks, the sourness on the faces of those who understood the change, the whispers, the sly smiles, all without any discretion. But no one and nothing could break her. Not anymore. She crossed oceans, cried through dawnless nights, and conquered borders and surgeries to stand there.

She was transforming into a beautiful butterfly, emerging from its cocoon day after day.

At night, before going to bed, she wrote a sentence in her new diary: I did it, I am myself, I love myself.

In the mornings, she would put on her lipstick in front of the mirror as a ritual, not as a makeshift disguise, but as a statement. Then she would let her gaze roll for a moment on her new idol, without smiling. She recognized it from the depths of her soul; that was enough for her.

Chiona often leaned her shoulder against the door frame of the room, staring at it from top to bottom. It was as if she were reading a poem that she didn't understand, but that moved her; this wasn't acceptance, it was something more substantial. It was unconditional love.

When her new identity arrived – with her name, gender, everything spelled correctly, everything as it should be Hope photographed it, put it in a small frame, and pinned it to the wall of her room. Right next to a small photo of her with her mother at the port, just before they left Casablanca.

Hope had already learned that freedom is not given, it is earned, it is claimed. She was about to turn twenty-two, but in her eyes, she had already lived two lives. She had decided to fight every day to be looked at. She wanted to be herself, but not a spectacle. There were times when she wondered whether she would ever have an everyday life, a job, friends, and love. She knew that the answer was not always straightforward. She had such a great need to be heard, but she was still afraid of being exposed. She wrote down new words in her notebook, the ones that women usually use. She tried to pronounce them with the appropriate tone, but she was not yet ready to say them out loud.

She experienced rejection by her father, his violence, and she experienced social stigmatization and marginalization. The choice to have the surgery in Casablanca ultimately shows that she had a strong will and courage within her.

This experience began to shape her character. She discovered that she could persevere, be patient, and be resilient in the face of difficulties. She certainly carried memories from before her mutation, perhaps even some traces of doubt or sadness. However, pride in what she had achieved prevailed.

In the first few days, she moved discreetly, but she observed everything. She kept Alexander's image alive within her. There were times when she felt him holding her hand, speaking softly in her ear, like back then, in the days of her great happiness.

She allowed herself only this image from the past to live in her soul.

Since she returned to Athens, she deliberately kept a distance from everyone. She was not yet completely ready. Not for her body, which, as time passed, became fuller and better. The hormone therapies worked wonders. It wasn't easy for someone to guess her previous identity.

One morning, passing in front of the detached house where the elderly couple lived, she felt Mrs. Penelope's gaze on her.

"My daughter, the woman said kindly, you look a lot like our Dimitros, who lives next door to the apartment building, and we have lost him for a long time now. We know that he has a sister, Anna, but we have not seen you. Are you related to him?"

Hope smiled and replied in a steady voice:

"No, you are wrong. I may have once looked like someone else, but now I look like me. Goodbye."

She usually woke up early in the morning, made a Greek coffee, and sat on the veranda. A little later, she would go to the local market, avoiding much conversation with everyone. She preferred a greengrocer who never asked anything.

She asked for acceptance without explanation.

She asked not to be asked to explain her past.

She asked for a home of her own, a community of people who wouldn't look at her strangely.

She asked for the right to be a woman, without always being the "trans" woman, a word she didn't consider her own.

The House In Pagrati

The months passed, arming herself with patience and strength. The hormone therapy was now entering its final stage. From a certain point on, a kind of maintenance for a considerable period was enough; then, the end.

Her genitals had been restored, and her figure and face depicted a brown, presentable woman. The length of her hair had well exceeded the height of her shoulders and descended like a brown waterfall down her back.

One warm afternoon, she stood in front of the mirror. The light of the setting sun gently bathed her face. She had traveled a long, difficult path until she reached the revolution of her youth, until the decision to be reborn in her own light, in Casablanca. There, for the first time, she touched the horizon and the air that was full of new promises; she acquired not only the body that belonged to her but also the right to a tomorrow without shame.

She realized that the time was approaching for the second big step: moving, a move she wanted not just to change her address, but to build her own home. Not the one they gave her, but the one she would choose herself.

She knew that going and leaving her mother and sister behind would not be easy. She loved them, but their love was no longer enough to keep her in a life that did not express her. Her 'suitcase' may have been small, but it was full of new dreams. She knew that she would receive pressure for her decision to leave, but she was ready to face it.

The move was not an escape. It was a return to herself, a step towards the life that she believed had always belonged to her.

More than a year and a half had passed since her surgery—a period of time filled with new rules of life, where Hope studied, getting excellent grades.

When she mentioned it to her family, she faced strong resistance from Chiona, but Hope was unconvinced.

Anna agreed more easily, but reluctantly. She was more understanding of her sister's needs. After a short marathon of reactions, she accepted it; in fact, she offered to help her get settled.

She gathered a few things: two or three favorite books, an old photo from Casablanca that reminded her of her birth, and a perfume that she had associated with that day, when she first walked as a woman in the sun.

The rest, she would find along the way. After all, what she carried in her soul was heavier and more precious than all the furniture in the world.

On the night of her departure, she stood and looked at her room for the last time. She left a letter on the table for her mother, who preferred not to be there that particular day. She had no anger, only gratitude.

Hope asked for nothing more than the right to be herself. And she got it herself.

A semi-basement furnished two-room apartment in Pagrati with some pots in the small uncovered space left by the previous tenant, her entire life.

The apartment was small and musty, but it fit her like a glove. She didn't want a view; she just wanted to hear herself.

The first few nights, she sat on a thick cushion that was Anna's, on the floor. She held a glass of cheap wine in her hand and dreamed of a life that spread her wings wide, the way she wanted it. She tried to fill the house with music, colors, and new friends. Maybe later, when she was ready, why not? And with love.

Here, in her new starting point, she began to rebuild, piece by piece, a life that had once seemed impossible to her. There were, of course, people who looked at her strangely, there were others who consciously avoided her, but there were also some — a few — who embraced her without asking questions.

She was desperately looking for a job. Prejudice against difference did not give her the right to equal opportunity, as a result of which doors were closed in her face before they even opened. In the end, how difficult it was!

She politely declined Nikolas's offer to return to the photo studio. It belonged to the past, and no matter how tempting the need was, she preferred to refuse.

In the spring of 1975, on Ermou Street, there was a small boutique full of clothes of a special aesthetic. A carefully cut piece of paper, discreetly affixed to the right side of the window, stated that the business was seeking a sales assistant.

Hope happened to be passing by, looking for a job in Athens. As soon as she read the ad, without wasting a moment, she gathered her courage and crossed the threshold.

Argyro, a bright, well-dressed fifty-something blonde with sparkling eyes, looked her over from top to bottom. The store smelled of expensive perfume. Before Hope could say a word, she asked her politely:

"Good morning, what can I do for you?"

Hope, confused, replied with shame coloring her cheeks:

"Yes, I saw in your window that you were looking for an employee. I really need to work."

"Do you have experience with clothes? Do you know anything about sewing?" Argyro asked.

"Unfortunately, not, but I have an appetite to learn. I'm a quick learner, you'll see. Please, give me a chance, you won't regret it. Are you the one in charge?"

Argyro looked at her in surprise. She was very nice to her. She understood from the first moment that she was trans; she did not comment on anything. She understood that the human being before her was fighting her own battle for survival in a complicated world, shaped by the life choice she had made.

She felt that she deserved a chance and decided to give it to her.

"Okay, then. But you have to do your best. You will start tomorrow for a while, and we will see how it goes. You may have to work extra hours, which I will not pay you, until you learn the job. You will be paid for six days' work at eight-hour intervals. As you understand, I am in charge! Are you happy?"

"Excited! Thank you very much, madam. I promise not to disappoint you."

In the first days of adaptation, time was timeless. The longing for creation burned like a fire in dry grass in Hope's soul.

Every day was different from the previous one and a harbinger of a better day to come. Finally, she felt as if she were joining a society that was supposed to repay her for all the harm it had done her; at least, that's what she believed.

Sometimes, during the lunch break, they would eat with Argyro in a picturesque tavern nearby. She was the first person outside her circle of friends that she trusted. And she didn't fall out. Argyro hugged her, sympathized with her, and offered her advice.

She was greatly lacking in the necessary accessories that characterize female coquetry, something her employer often took care to cover up with diligence. Hope talked to her about everyone and everything. Argyro became not only her boss but also her good friend. They communicated with Chiona infrequently and spoke with Anna by phone twice or three times, without any special conversations.

One Step, One Friend, Lina

Shortly before Christmas, one morning when Argyro was away on business, a young lady crossed the threshold of the boutique. She was wearing a tight black dress and high heels. Elegant, with a stern hat and a demeanor that indicated that she couldn't stand many looks. She stood in front of the counter. Her voice was calm, her age around thirty. She leaned her bag on a chair while casting a searching look at Hope.

"Good morning, I would like something special, she said, and paused. They told me that here you know about different bodies."

Hope looked at her carefully, but politely.

"Good morning," she said, smiling meaningfully. "If the body has a history, then yes, we do. What size do you wear?"

"My name is Lina. Have you ever been told that your eyes remind you of '60s movies?"

"I am Hope. Yes, some people told me."

Lina took her bag from the chair, placed it on the bench, and took a step closer to her.

"Paris, 1965. Honor and risk. You?"

Hope, more collected:

"Casablanca 1973. Medicine and silence."

Lina looks at her deeply, almost tenderly.

"And yet you are here, whole", she tells her.

"Only when someone like you sees me," Hope replies, looking her in the eyes.

The two women stand facing each other, as if, in a few seconds, they will recognize the lives that carry decades of struggle.

Lina breaks the silence:

"I would like, Hope, to sew a suit, a beautiful red suit. Is it possible?"

"Of course it is possible! Our hands will sew it together with our souls."

"Will I have time to have it before New Year's?" Lina asked with a smile. "The shop where I work is having a New Year's Eve party, and I would really like to wear it."

"Mrs. Argyro will tell you that. She will come in a little while; do you want to wait for her?"

"Yes, I have some time. Besides, she should take my measurements!" Lina said, smiling, self-mockingly, while making an almost dance-like movement with her right hand to show her height.

"Really, Lina, what do you do? You've piqued my curiosity."

"I work at Velvet, my dear, do you know that?"

"Unfortunately, no. Do you want to tell me?"

"It's a big bar on Patission Street. I'm a barmaid there. Come one night, I'll treat you. I think you'll like it."

Hope nodded, looking Lina in the eye. Her air, her appearance, her confidence, her eloquence, everything had won her over. This young woman had a strange influence on her. Perhaps she represented everything she wanted. One thing was sure: she admired her greatly, even though she had only just met her.

Argyro entered her shop a little later, clearly irritated.

"You shouldn't go to these public services; they bother you for no reason," she said and left the bag of papers she was carrying in her office.

"Hope, did you serve the lady?" she asked, looking at Lina.

"We were waiting for you, Ms. Argyro. She wants to sew a suit and wonders if she will have time to wear it on New Year's Eve. Are we in time for her?"

"We will do something, Hope. No customer leaves here complaining."

"Great!" Lina exclaimed, clapping her hands happily. "When do we start, Ms. Argyro?"

"Even now, if you have time. Do you have time?"

"Of course, take advantage of me while you can!" Lina replied, laughing happily.

"Hope, lead the lady to the studio. I'll be there in five minutes!"

CHAPTER FIVE

THE UNEXPECTED THREAT

The Past Return

One Tuesday evening, a few days after meeting Lina, Hope returned tired from work to her semi-basement house. A white envelope, with no sender, thrown under the closed door, made its appearance.

The strange thing was that she wasn't expecting anything from anyone. No one even knew her address, except for Anna. Who could have sent it?

The invisible fear of the unknown ran down her spine, sending shivers. She opened the envelope, turning on the lamp's low light at the same time. Inside was only a poorly taken photo of her under the Acropolis, when she worked with Nikolas. She was wearing men's clothes and sitting outside a tavern with high stone windowsills, in Plaka. Alexander had taken this photo; she remembered it well. But how had it reached the sender's hands? She never learned that. Her old name was written in pen on the back: Dimitros, 1971.

She collapsed in fright on the worn-out sofa, not knowing what to assume.

She had been restless all night; she could not close her eyes. The look on her face the next day revealed the difficult night she had spent, something that did not go unnoticed by Argyro. When she asked her what was wrong with her, Hope limited herself to saying she was a little unwell and that this prevented her from sleeping.

Argyro didn't believe her, but contented herself with patting her motherly on the head, telling her to be careful, and that by tomorrow she would be fine.

Another envelope, again anonymous, appeared under her door the same way after four days, upsetting her even more. It contained a photograph at Keratsini, taken from a distance, showing the entrance to the apartment building. On the back, it read: Hope, 1973. Someone must know, she thought. Someone is watching her. But who?

Her mind was frozen; she had no idea. She had never hurt anyone. Why are they doing this to her? What do they want from her?

She avoided discussing it; she didn't want to embarrass anyone. She understood that the person sending her the photos wasn't just a threat; it was someone who knew her very well. Someone who was planning something for her, without her knowledge.

Her heart was beating strangely. Who could have these photos? They weren't there anymore; she had burned them all, or so she thought.

Hope must now dig back into the past that she had worked so hard to overcome. To search for people she had left behind. Someone she knew from her village? A relative who never forgave her for the change? But who? Could it be someone from the past? Someone who met her in Casablanca? Or maybe someone closer. Someone who sees her now?

The semi-basement became a prison. The silence Hope had sought turned into a trap. The sounds from the apartment next door seemed like breaths over her shoulder.

Someone knew her better than she thought. And they were speaking to her through silent messages.

And then came the third letter. A final blow in the form of a note this time: *We live in hope. But you, Hope, you will die soon.*

Velvet was lit mainly by multi-colored lamps with amber light. The walls had wallpaper with geometric patterns and metal details. Shades of orange, brown, and gold dominated. Some scattered touches of burgundy complemented the decoration. Mirrors on the walls and columns visually enlarged the space and added a sense of shine.

The seats were low and upholstered in velvet. The tables were round, with a varnished wooden surface and thin metal legs.

Behind the bar, the bottles on the shelves were arranged haphazardly, illuminated by discreet soft lighting. Smoking was a common habit; there were half-full ashtrays everywhere. The aroma of tobacco mixed with the smells of drinks and the perfumes of the customers. All together they weighed down the atmosphere.

The patrons were rather poorly dressed. A riot of colors had its place. Men wore jackets, wide ties, and shirts with wide open collars. Women wore psychedelic dresses or skirts that looked like wide belts, and t-shirts in bright colors, accompanied by shoes, mainly platforms. Of course, there was no shortage of large earrings.

When Hope entered Velvet, Gloria Gaynor was singing 'I Will Survive' on the speakers. She loved that song very much; she had identified it with her life.

Lina, at that moment, was serving a customer at the other end of the bar, but she saw Hope and motioned for her to sit near her. The two of them had found each other; it wasn't the first time she had been there. She was the only one who knew the envelopes existed. She advised her to keep her mouth shut until the sender revealed himself. She thought he had a purpose in threatening her. There was no reason for someone to kill her, for something she might have done without her knowledge in the past. She sat on a high velvet stool with an iron back, in the corner of the bar, with her back against the wall.

"How are you, my dear, today? A little better? Do we have something new?"

"No, Lina, I don't have anything. But I'm terrified, I keep moving forward and looking behind me. I can't take it anymore."

"Didn't I tell you to be patient? The culprit will appear. He will. What can I get you to drink now, to relax?"

"Something light, please. You know I don't drink much."

"Okay. Are you okay with a glass of white wine?"

"Yes, it's fine!"

Soon, with a glass of white wine in one hand and the coaster in the other, Lina approached her friend.

"Enjoy it and don't rush. I have a little work to do, I'll be back in a bit, okay?"

"I'm not going anywhere, I'll wait for you," she replied with a smile.

In front of the bar, Hope was trying to look calm. She

was secretly licking her lips, so that they wouldn't crack from the dryness of fear.

At the other end of the bar, a man in his fifties was sitting. He was wearing a beige shirt with sleeves rolled up to his elbows. His eyes never closed! He had been watching her from the moment she set foot in the bar. He was drinking alone, without company. At one point, he got up and approached her.

"What's your name?" he asked.

Hope smiled slightly.

"Is that necessary?" she replied politely.

"I didn't ask if you have savings in the bank, I just asked to know your name. You're gorgeous... for a man."

Silence. Full of embarrassment, she squeezed her glass tightly.

"Don't get confused. I'm not a man, sir."

The man smiled, with a smile that had no humor at all.

"Do you want to discuss this more privately? I know where 'good' girls like you go when they get tired of being alone."

Before she could answer, Lina abruptly approached them.

"Give us a break, Mitso. Leave her alone. Can't you see that she doesn't know you?"

Mitsos laughed, loudly this time.

"Everyone knows me, my sweet. Ask your boss."

He greeted her gravely and left like a shadow. Hope was trembling, but she didn't show it.

Lina turned and whispered to her:

"He is the reason why many girls have disappeared.

Don't ever sit near him. And if you ever meet him again and he invites you for a drink, say that you are fasting for Saint Paisios."

It was past two when she left Velvet. She felt stressed and exhausted. This whole story about the anonymous letters upset the delicate balance she had worked so hard to establish within herself. When she left the bar, she noticed that a car with foreign license plates had started following her. At first, she thought it was a coincidence. She turned right, then left, but it continued to follow her, carefully, from a distance.

She turns sharply, and the car stops abruptly, too.

Terrified, she runs. But someone blocks her way.

"Don't shout, it's no good. Get in the car."

In the back seat, two men in black clothes with their faces covered. One gets out, and before she can get in, he hits her in the stomach with something heavy. She's out of breath. She tries to escape, but he pulls her by the hair and throws her into the back seat. Hope screams. One of them puts his hand in her mouth.

"Do you want to stay with your teeth? Shut up, or I'll break them."

They leave the center and drive towards Ano Petralona, avoiding the main roads and taking dirt roads. They cross some railway tracks and arrive at an old, half-destroyed factory.

They pull her out. They literally drag her. They throw her into a room with a dirty concrete floor. A hanging storm lamp flickers on one side. A man takes a chair and sits in front of her.

The darkness hides him; his back is turned to the lamp.

Hope is shaking with fear. She coughs. She has been through all this before; she remembers it. You don't forget the nightmares.

"I wrote to you, you will die," he tells her sharply in broken Greek.

"But why? What have I done to you? Who are you?" she asks him, trembling with fear.

"Does the name Christos remind you of anything, you scumbag?"

The blood froze in her veins. A knot formed in her throat, making it difficult to breathe and making her voice disappear. "Christos?" she mumbled with difficulty.

"Yes, Christos. The one you and the whore in Troumba sent to prison."

"But... he... "

"Since your ass wanted it, you stupid scumbag, you drank it together. He is now in the dirt, while you are living your new life. I am his brother. He managed to tell me, before they killed him in jail. We have been looking for you for months now. Fortunately, your gang has rats.

Hope stopped crying; she no longer shouted; she looked at her destiny with sadness."

"No one will look for you. You were wrong from the moment you were born."

He hit her once, twice, three times; in the mouth, in the stomach, and he tore her eyebrow. She was bleeding nonstop. The man was laughing loudly, holding in his right hand a sharp blade that gleamed in the faint light, ready to plunge it into her body.

Hope saw it. Inside, she was begging him to finish quickly. In a heartbreaking voice, she told him:

"Don't be late, you asshole... kill me, and we're done."

Before anything bad could happen, a loud noise shook the walls of the old factory. From the back, lights turned the night into day. Someone was honking loudly, not once but continuously. It sounded like a siren, but it was a truck horn.

The man panicked. His two henchmen got out to see what was happening, while the truck driver and his passenger started shouting:

"Hey, what are you doing in there, you bums? I'll call the police!"

In the chaos, Hope crawled, found a rusty iron, and hit the man in the knee with all the strength she had left. She shouted:

"Here! Help! I'm here!"

The driver heard her first. Both men entered the room, one holding a flashlight, the other a baseball bat. The others, seeing the newcomers determined for everything, fled. The man who was holding her was writhing in pain and limped away. They all got into the car and disappeared.

The driver looked at her in horror.

"Jesus Christ... Wait, girl, we'll take you to the hospital."

The next day, Hope woke up in Laiko Hospital. She had bruises and stitches, but she was breathing. She was alive, and that was the main thing.

The driver, an old trucker who took goods with his assistant to Rouf, told the police officers who questioned him:

"I always stop when I pass by there. It's dark and quiet. After so many hours at the wheel, it's good to pee. This time, however, things were very different..."

Was it a miracle? Or a second chance? Who knows.

When Hope came to, he was near her. She gratefully took his hand.

"Thank you for saving me. And that's enough for me", she told him.

A nurse enters the room, holding a vial of serum.

"Hope, are you in pain? Can I get you something?" she asked formally.

"I'm in pain, but I don't want anything more. Thank you."

"Would you like to talk to a doctor? Maybe a psychologist?"

"Why would I do that, sister? Do I seem crazy?"

Hope's response was so abrupt and aggressive that the nurse felt uncomfortable.

"I didn't say anything like that, forgive me. I thought that, after what happened, you might need it."

Hope, who had her eyes fixed on the ceiling, nervously lowered her head and looked her straight in the face.

"I don't need a psychologist, you hear? I need a day without fear. I need a mirror that doesn't see me as a problem. I need a word that fits me. You hear?"

And then a tear fell first, then another, and then it didn't stop.

Hope curled up in bed like a wounded beast. Her body was wrapped in a white sheet, but it didn't warm her. Her body was frozen.

Her fingers gently touch her neck. She feels nothing.

But it hurts, and that means it still exists.

She is delirious: If I don't feel, I am safe.

She closed her eyes. Loud voices returned.

Not the men's. She saw her mother, her father, and the village.

They were shouting:

It is not a child. It is our shame.

This thing will not bear my name.

And then, silence.

She had wanted to fix her body so that they would be silent.

But now, her body betrayed her. It hurt, but she wasn't angry.

She was ashamed that it was hers.

The curtain creaked from the ventilation. Every creak seemed to say: You are still alive.

She didn't sleep. She waits.

The next morning, she was sitting in bed with her back slightly raised.

Her face was bruised, her gaze downcast, full of confusion. She covered her mouth and jaw with the corner of the sheet.

The door to the room opened slowly, without a sound, as if she didn't want to disturb the silence. Hope turned her head sharply, her eyes burning with insomnia and fear. For a moment, she froze; after the night before last, every shadow was now a threat to her. But the figure that entered the room was not threatening in the least. It was Lina. Tall, with loose hair, tight jeans, and a black coat, wet on the shoulders from the morning summer rain. She stood in the doorway, her gaze soft and hard at the same time.

It was hidden anger, slowly bubbling up beneath the affection. Anger for what had happened, because she herself had experienced something similar a few years ago.

"I've been looking for you since yesterday," he said softly, without coming closer to her. "Thank goodness you gave the truck driver the shop's phone number, and he called me. He came from the shop last night and told me everything, in every detail."

Hope didn't speak, but her eyes filled with that mixed relief that only a kindred spirit could understand.

Then Lina took the first step, closing the door behind her. She slowly approached the bed and pulled a chair next to her.

"What did they do to you, my little one?"

Hope answered with difficulty and a broken voice:

"I don't... I don't know. I didn't have time to. It was... it was just, I left you, and they were waiting for me."

She stopped talking and bit her lips.

"You don't have to tell me anything. Now I'm here with you."

And she reached out to gently hold her hand.

"I'm afraid, Lina. What if they come back? What if they look for me? I don't know where to go."

In the background, the light from the window dimly

illuminated the room, creating a strange feeling between freedom and prison.

Without the slightest hesitation, Lina answered:

"You'll come with me, I'm not discussing it. You will stay with me as long as necessary. I will take you to where I work. Everyone will respect you. No one will bother you. No one will look at you the wrong way."

There was a resounding determination in Lina's gaze. He was there to support her, to offer her security, to give her a new beginning.

"But what am I supposed to do there? I'm a mess. I don't even know if I can stand up, let alone..." Lina interrupted her gently, confidently, and lovingly.

"You won't come there to work. You'll come to get back on your feet. For me to take care of you. To remember who you are. And when you're ready, then you decide."

Hope looked at her with complete gratitude.

"But I'm not strong, like you," she replied with a secret sob.

"Neither was I, when someone like us reached out to me. Come on, let's do it together."

In Velvet Club

The lighting at Velvet was not dimmed; it was too early for that.

Soft funk music generously provided tones of calm.

Hope stood for a moment at the entrance, looking around with reservation. In the past summer months, she had fully recovered but had not left Lina's house, where she had been staying since her discharge. Even these, her personal belongings from the apartment in Pagrati, were brought to her by her friend.

Fear embroidered forms of death in every cell of her body. In vain did Chiona and Anna try to bring her back to the safety of home, in Keratsini.

She quit her job at Argyro, of course, after first thanking her with gratitude for what she had offered her.

The time had come to try to live again, whatever that entailed. The endless hours of discussions with Lina and a friend of hers, a psychologist, finally gave her the impetus to start over, no matter how difficult it seemed. It was now imperative to leave the darkness behind and find a crack of light.

Today was her first night at the bar. She would work as a waitress, though she didn't make much money. Under Lina's constant pressure, she had agreed to work with her.

Besides, her options had evaporated. She felt her friend's presence offering her the reassurance she so desperately needed.

Lina, behind the bar, spotted her as soon as she entered. She called out loudly, raising her hand, and ran to greet her:

"Hope! Here I am, my sweetie. Break a leg, isn't that what they usually call it?" she said jokingly.

"Yes, my friend, that's what they call it. I hope this time it comes true."

Hope stepped forward a little hesitantly. She looked around, as if to make sure she was welcome. It's more beautiful than I expected, she thought.

Lina was holding the towel she used behind the bar.

"The first time is always a bit difficult, but you'll be with me, and no one bothers my queen."

She smiled timidly, clearly moved.

"I don't know if I feel ready, but I'll try not to disappoint you."

"Come on, leave that for now, my dear, come and let me introduce you to our boss."

Antonis was standing behind the bar and in front of the cash register, rummaging through something in its open drawer. He was wearing tight black jeans and a black leather vest over a navy shirt. His hair was very short, which put him out of step with the times. Although his facial features were not harsh, his gaze said precisely the opposite.

When the two friends approached, he fixed his gaze on Hope.

"I remember you," he told her.

"She had come a few months ago, two or three times," Lina rushed to speak. "I talked to you, Antonis, about what happened."

"Yes, yes; welcome, then. I was pleased. Hope, did you say your name?"

"Yes, Hope. I was pleased too," she replied.

"We will have a good collaboration, don't worry. Everything will go well. Lina will show you the way around, and we will start."

"Thank you very much, Antonis. I will do my best!"

"Time will tell, my dear," he replied, leaving a hidden implication to wander in the space.

The evenings passed, giving Hope time to get to know

the people who, overcome by alcohol, poured out their innermost feelings. Most, thirsty with sadness, were looking for a safe harbor to anchor for a few hours before starting their stormy journey through life again.

The two friends were late waking up each time.

Sometimes, from the continuous night out, they would open their eyes early in the afternoon, just enough to drink a coffee, get ready, and go to the bar. They managed the bullock and scrambled everything, sharing the household's needs.

Two or three months later, after she had acclimated to the Velvet environment, Hope began to sometimes cover for the barmaid who had taken the day off.

One night while she was working behind the bar, a drunken patron approached her. When he realized that she was trans, he became threatening. At first, he tried to kiss her by pulling her hand. She refused intelligently, without offending him, something he did not do. He started cursing her rudely in front of everyone.

Lina then intervened to protect her, and tension arose.

Antonis did not take a position. He remained in his corner at the counter, enjoying his drink. A little later, when the customer left, angry that he was not having his fun, the mood calmed down. As soon as Lina left, Antonis approached Hope. She leaned a little so that she could hear her boss, and he said to her in a low, calm tone:

"Be more of a kitty cat; nothing would happen if he kissed you. We want customers like that; then whatever they take out, they will put it here. You took out your nails;

that's not how it works, do you understand?"

Lina, who was watching from the other corner of the bar, lit a cigarette and waved at her.

Hope approached her, clearly troubled.

"Don't talk to them too much, and if they ask you questions, pretend to listen. You smile at them, without continuing. Unless you want to make more money... "

"What do you mean by 'make more money'? I don't understand what you mean."

"Listen, Hope, there's something I haven't told you. Of course, the final decision will be yours."

"What have you hidden from me? Tell me, what? What decision should I make or not? Don't scare me, please."

"Don't act like that, you idiot. Some gentlemen need an escort outside the club."

"So what?"

"Any girl who wants, she goes. They pay well. If they want more, they stay overnight with them. Antonis arranges this after asking the girl first."

"Have you done it?" Hope asked, eyes wide open.

"Several times. Men I liked have passed by. Why should I say no?"

"But that's it like... I'm ashamed even to say it!"

"It's nothing. Clear things. And I have my peace. I don't believe in love and affection, my friend. I used to believe, but not anymore. Look what you pulled when you trusted. Everybody just wants to fuck. So now, I'm fucking them."

Hope, stunned and with a knot choking her, returned to her post without saying a word. Lina's words whirled like manic satellites in her mind. She realized that, up to a point, she was right. This scared her even more. The truth is, after so long, she missed male company. She was young, she craved hugs, caresses, a man's scent, love. She changed so many things with pain and perseverance. She suffered to obtain what, unfortunately, was not blooming.

Yes, but for a fee?

They didn't exchange another word all night. Lina didn't leave with her that night; Antonis left her outside their door.

It was past four. Hope didn't turn on all the lights, only the small one in the bathroom. She took off her heels and left them in the hallway, as if she couldn't bear their weight anymore. She threw some ice water on her face. She looked in the mirror.

There she was, there was the image she had painstakingly built in the operating rooms. She remembered the tears, the expectations, the hopes. Beautiful, pure, and yet alone. Almost empty. Lina had said: Look what you pulled when you trusted.

Yes, she had been hurt. She had felt the rejection and violence like a slap. And yet, how much had not been said about her, after they had first used her.

Lina was sleeping. With her pillow in her arms, she had entered into a safe embrace, that of Morpheus.

The next day, Hope woke up early. She waited for a little while for the time to pass. Around noon, with two mugs of steaming coffee in her hand, she knocked gently on Lina's door.

"Come in," her voice sounded sleepy.

"I don't know if I can see someone like this, but... I want to try. I want to see if someone can touch me. To see me, not as a fantasy, but as a person, she told her sharply. And she continued: "Just one date, okay? Let me see what it's like. But I want to choose who I see. And I want to be safe."

Lina looked at her with a mixture of surprise and seriousness.

"That's how it should be, Hope. And that's how it will be. But first, say good morning to me and smile a little."

A smile was born on her lips, similar to that of a student who wrote well in an exam, without having read. A smile that hid anticipation deep down.

The First Date

Michael entered the bar and sat across from Hope. He ordered his drink, ending the conversation with just a polite "Thank you." Nothing else. He was clearly staring at her the entire time she was there. At one point, he motioned to Antonis, said something quietly, and left silently, just as he had come. When Antonis later spoke to her about Michael, she asked him, with her hands sweating incessantly, what exactly he wanted.

"He wants to meet you... That."

"Only?" she asked, puzzled.

"Have a coffee with him, and we'll see," he replied curtly.

Three days later, Antonis set up her first date.

The man was waiting for her at a cocktail bar in Koukaki. Antonis had only told her his name: Michael. He was, he said, "A nice guy."

They didn't even talk about "guarantees." He just wanted to get to know her.

That afternoon, her stomach was in knots. She had changed three dresses before settling on the simple black one, the one she liked because it hugged her body without being a public pilgrimage. She put on a little perfume; something discreet, almost timid. Her hands were shaking a little as she bought a bus ticket.

Entering the bar, she saw him. In the daylight, she could tell his age. He was around forty. Michael recognized her immediately. He got up from his chair politely to welcome her.

"I'm so glad you came," he told her with a smile.

"Me too," Hope whispered.

She didn't know whether to shake his hand or sit down.

At first, they chatted about indifferent things - movies, traveling. Michael discreetly avoided looking at her beautiful body, which he liked so much. He didn't like the rabid looks with cheap interest. Something she wanted but also confused her.

Hope looked him straight in the eye. She took a big sip of her cocktail to gain courage and asked him sharply, as Lina had taught her.

"You know that... I'm a trans woman, right?"

He leaned back, calm.

"Yes, I know," he said. I came because I just wanted to meet you. Not because I'm attracted to something strange. I'm interested in you."

Her heart beat strangely. Maybe out of relief. Maybe out of fear. She always expected the insult. He didn't say anything like, I'm interested, but I can't. Too bad, you're very pretty, but it doesn't work for me.

They talked for hours. Then they went out together and walked for a little while. Michael asked her, holding her hand, if she wanted to continue to the hotel. She stood for a moment, looking at him.

"I want to, but you know I'm scared. I've never been like this before.

"When you say 'like this', what do you mean?"

"To go with someone who sees me a little more clearly."

He didn't believe her; he smiled at her with his mouth closed, without commenting on anything.

In the hotel room, he held her hands and kissed her gently. He took off her dress carefully. He touched her, as she asked, not with greed, but with acceptance. He didn't ask questions. He didn't search her body as if exploring a mystery. Then, they lay down side by side.

Michael was sleeping peacefully. Hope was looking at him, not sure whether she should feel strong or exposed. But she had to return to the bar.

She got something from this date, besides the envelope of money. Something small, a sense that she was capable of being loved, even a little, in this way. She didn't feel complete; not everything was resolved. The void was there; it remained. But perhaps it was a little shallow now.

CHAPTER SIX

WITH A DEVASTATED SOUL

Dangerous Loves

Lina was waiting for her in a room at the back of the store that Antonis used as a wine cellar. Sitting on a rickety chair, she slowly drank her coffee, smoking one cigarette after another furiously.

As soon as Hope entered, with a look that revealed more than she could say, she asked her:

"How did it go?"

Hope didn't answer; she left her bag on the table and sat down across from her. She only gave her an empty sidelong look, and then silence.

"Okay, I won't ask you. But... be careful."

"There's nothing to watch out for anymore," she replied, troubled, breaking her silence. The evening passed as if it were a silent film. The customers' touches didn't bother her like they used to, because she no longer let them reach inside her. Their phrases, their compliments, their cheap "baby" seemed funny to her. Everything changed in the blink of an eye, as if they had become a smokescreen.

Two days later, Antonis set up a second date for her, then a third, a fourth... The fifth was a blind date.

Hope reacted, but temporarily. The baton of persuasion went into Lina's hands. She reassured her, saying that he was one of her best customers. She assured her that she had also gone with him before.

Antonis had given her the name of the hotel and the

room number, no other description, just instructions.

"It'll be simple. Don't worry," Antonis told her.

She arrived at the hotel ten minutes later.

She didn't want to seem eager for everything. Nor punctual. Nor anything.

When she knocked on the door, a tall middle-aged man with tired eyes opened it. Michael was already in the room, wearing only his trousers. He didn't shake her hand, he didn't say good evening, he just made room for her to pass inside. Hope entered without uttering a word.

"Do you want something to drink?" He asked her as he closed the door.

"No. Let's finish."

Michael stood still for a few seconds, looking at her. Then, he nodded. Hope took off her blouse herself. Then, clumsily, mechanically, she unbuttoned his trousers. There were no words, no games, no flirting. There was no feeling. Only "action." She turned her back on him for a moment, when they were finished, to hide a tear. She got up, almost running, and locked herself in the bathroom. She washed herself hastily. She put her clothes back on and left, taking the money from the bedside table. She took it without remorse. She stood in the doorway for a few seconds.

"You won't see me again," she told him calmly, without looking. Michael didn't answer.

She took the stairs instead of taking the elevator. Her feet felt heavy, but her mind was at peace. She had no more doubts. There were no feelings to be hurt: just an act, an agreement, an exchange.

It was drizzling outside. Hope walked to the stop. The

air smelled of wet cement. I'm surviving, she thought. That's enough. Nothing more.

Returning to the bar, she was even more different, not stronger, but definitely altered. The defense mechanism had been activated, and her body was there, but something deeper had now withdrawn, leaving a darker sense of detachment.

Before she got to work behind the bar, she visited the bathroom. She looked at her face in the mirror. No, it wasn't new or old.

The image was a shell, a presence. A "yes" that no longer had consequences.

Antonis passed by the bar later. He approached her, motioning to bend down to tell her. As soon as Hope bent down, he whispered in her ear:

"Michael wasn't happy. But if you want, I have another one."

Hope tilted her head slightly.

"I'll tell you tomorrow."

She already knew what she would tell him. She would tell him whatever he wanted to hear. She didn't feel. And when you don't feel, anything is allowed.

She felt betrayed by Lina. She had been betrayed by herself, not her friend. Everything had begun to develop in such a way that she realized that if she continued, she might lose control. Yes, she was following the choice Lina suggested, but the moment she decided to do so, fear in her soul took over. A fear of death overshadowed her needs. She knew very well that the contract that Christos' brother had with her was pending. She was sure that, at some point, he would find her again, but she didn't know when.

If this hadn't happened, there was no way she would have left Argyro's shop or her semi-basement house. She didn't even dare to communicate with her own people, for fear of involving them. She especially didn't want that at all.

The rift between the two friends grew over time, not only at work but also in their personal lives. Lina, who had started down this path long before, believed she was in control. Now, however, she saw Hope sinking day by day, maintaining a frozen silence that scared her.

One evening, after a few months, Hope had gone out for a cigarette in the back alley of the shop. She felt the need to be alone for a few minutes. She didn't smoke before. But now, she liked this bitterness in her mouth. It cut the sweetness out of the lie.

Lina came after her, hastily buttoning her jeans. Someone had pulled her into a dressing room for a quickie sex. She was sweaty, her face red, and a bit lost.

"Hope, can I talk to you for a moment?"

Hope took a long drag on her cigarette and, without looking at her, replied:

"Speak. What do you have to say to me? I'm listening to you."

"Don't fuck with me, I just don't know what you're doing lately, you're constantly getting lost. Even when you're here, you're missing. You act like nothing's your business."

Hope stubbed out her cigarette forcefully against the wall, clearly irritated.

"Listen, maybe this is the trick. Didn't you teach me not to care about anything? Did you forget it?"

"It's not a trick, Hope, what's happening to you. It's a loss, I can see it in your eyes. You have nothing inside you anymore. Not pain, not joy, nothing. It's like you've become a ghost."

Hope turned and looked at her with a cold gaze.

"What's wrong with you? Didn't you tell me that's how it happens? Clear things, without love, without pink fantasies. You said: they only want to fuck me. Well, I give them what they want. That's it."

"Yes, but I didn't say you should die inside to do it." Lina's voice had broken.

Hope looked at her emotionlessly. She didn't know how to feel remorse. There was no room for that.

"Don't lecture me, Lina, do you hear? I followed in your footsteps, I took your path, I'm just taking it further than you can bear."

Lina fell silent. She knew it; she had seen it. Hope was something else now. Not a girl trying to endure. But a girl who had stopped caring. The expropriation of her soul was now blatant.

A light came on at the back of the shop. Antonis came out too.

"Hope, a customer is asking about you. Do you want it or not?"

Hope didn't even look at Lina.

"Yes. Tell him, I'm available." She went inside without saying another word.

Lina stayed outside. For the first time, she was afraid

for her, but also for herself. Because, through Hope, he saw the end of their journey.

Three days after the verbal incident with her friend, Antonis approached her at her post.

"Let's have a couple of drinks together, Hope."

"Are we cut loose today when we don't have work, boss?

"For you, my star, there will always be! You know, we have some clients who ask for escorts for more exclusive phases. Clean jobs. Cash in hand. You have an air that bends iron. Do you want it?"

Hope didn't answer immediately. She had learned to buy time.

"If it's clean, yes, why not?" She told him after a while.

Antonis gave her a folded piece of paper.

"Today, at eleven, be there. Dress nicely, and don't tell anyone."

The address was somewhere in Kolonaki. She went to a point by bus. Then on foot, walking. Her mood for what she would encounter was clearly enigmatic on her face. A detached house with an old, heavy wooden door. A bell with no name on the right pillar. She pressed it without the slightest hesitation. It opened a small window that was on the door. Someone with a well-groomed beard and a small cut on her cheek opened the door, without asking her who she was or what she wanted. She entered.

The same guy showed her a wooden staircase that creaked as she climbed it. At the end of it was a wide, worn hallway with dark gray carpeting, and a ceiling light on the wall that barely illuminated it. A shiver ran through her body.

Some room in the back had a door half-open, through which rays of pulsating red light escaped. Something like a beacon of danger. Inside, men in suits, cigars, colognes heavy as oil. Women dressed, painted, quiet, not all trans, but most with broken faces.

One, very young, approached her.

"Is this your first time here?"

"Yes. You?"

"Listen, there's no second. Either you leave now, tonight, or you stay forever."

The first man who approached her, before she could find out anything, was around sixty. He smiled at her with straight, fake teeth. He seemed to have authority, from the way the others looked at him.

"Come on, let's have a drink," he said to her through his teeth.

Hope accepted, and she sat down opposite him.

"You're probably one of the new ones. Who sent you here?"

"Antonis."

"Oh, actually, Antonis... He only sends us good things, may my friend be well. Well done, you, my girl, are a complete package. I'll be John to you."

The answer was a trap. Hope understood and didn't answer; she just smiled at him.

"It doesn't matter. The only thing that matters is that your face isn't broken yet. I like that."

A scream was heard from behind a closed door—a girl, with a scream that would break a glass. No one reacted. Not even the man. It's as if they were used to it.

Hope stood up.

"I'm sorry. I think I made a mistake. I have to leave."

The man gently grabbed her wrist.

"Not yet, my dear. Some asked her for something, and she refused. You're not like that, so don't be afraid, here with me, you're safe," the man said, winking at her slyly. And he continued: "Here you don't refuse, and the world rolls at your feet. If you say no, you leave. Remember, though, not all of them leave standing."

The words he uttered sounded like a threat.

She realized then that it was human trafficking. There were girls locked in rooms. And then, for the first time, she wasn't afraid; she was angry.

She couldn't do anything else, except run away, indifferent to the consequences. Chatting for a while with the sixty-year-old man, she managed to convince him that she was ready for anything. At the right moment, as he exchanged a few words with others, she bent down, cleverly took her high-heeled shoes in one hand and her soul in the other, and before they knew what was happening, she was already on the street.

Her heart was about to break, her legs ached unbearably, and she didn't turn to look back. She had the impression that everyone was chasing her. She arrived, running nonstop, at Syntagma. She was shaking from the panic that had taken over every cell of her body. What consequences would this have? Would they be looking for her? She couldn't think straight. She hailed a taxi. She gave him Lina's address. It was all she could think about. When she got to the house, she quickly went inside and locked the door. Lina would logically be at the bar. She would call her to tell her, yes, that's what she would do. She threw away everything she was wearing; her clothes stank of misery. She went into the bathroom and let the icy water run over her sweaty body.

Wrapped in a full-length towel, she sat on a kitchen chair. The phone was on the wall across from her. She picked up the receiver, stretching the cord. She dialed the bar phone. She rang several times until she heard Lina's familiar voice.

"It's me, she told her in a trembling voice."

"Where are you? What happened? Antonis is furious!"

"I went to the house he told me about."

"Why didn't you tell me? I wouldn't let you go. Girls have gone missing there. They don't exist anymore. And no one is looking for them."

"I didn't know, I didn't expect it. What do I do now? I'm scared!"

"Try to calm down. I'll go in your place, I've been there before. I'll see you when I get back. Get some rest."

"Antonis?"

"I'll calm him down, don't worry."

"Be careful, Lina, please. Thank you!"

The Disappearance.

An endless night of nightmares, slowly gnawing away at the hours of her life, until the sunlight decided to make darkness disappear. Hope had not closed her eyes for a single minute. Curled up once more in a corner of the bed, she patiently awaited Lina's arrival.

But Lina was nowhere to be seen. Nine, ten, eleven; not a single phone call. Her instinct foretold that something bad had happened. I'll go to the bar, she thought. If she doesn't show up by the afternoon, I'll go to the bar.

Antonis will know where she's gotten herself into.

That evening, when she entered the bar, she realized that her boss was missing. He didn't go behind the bar to work; he sat in a corner waiting for him.

Around twelve o'clock, she saw him cross the threshold.

"Antonis," she called out to him, raising her hand. He looked at her, for a moment, with a mixture of coldness and indifference. Then, he nodded his head to let her know that he had seen her. In a few minutes, he approached her and sat down in the chair opposite her.

"I hear you. What do you want? You have a lot of nerve to show up. You made me look bad in front of the client. It's a shame, and I trusted you. You ruined everything, you have no place here anymore!"

"Lina hasn't come back yet, Antonis. Where did you send her? Where is she?" she replied angrily.

"And how do you want me to know? She's a big girl; she knows how to be careful."

"If she doesn't come by tomorrow, you know I'm going to the police."

"Are you threatening me?"

"I'm warning you."

"Get off my back, Hope. Your best friend might have found somewhere better. She might have left suddenly. How should I know? Am I her protector?"

Lina's coat, however, was still hanging on the hanger. She had seen it, going to the bathroom earlier, as she was waiting for him. She said nothing more. She looked at him angrily and hurried away. She was now sure that someone had "transported" Lina or "disappeared" her for the knowledge and compliance of the other girls.

On the way back, a storm of thoughts choked her. What should she do? If I don't speak, she thought, maybe no one will talk. But if I do, they will bury me before they even know my name. Did she have to choose between keeping quiet, surviving, and dealing with an entire system? Hope, however, was angry, an anger that defeated her fears.

The next morning, she went to the police. She kept alive in her the hope that her friend would be found. The policeman at the gate asked her what she wanted. When she told him she wanted to report a missing person, he led her to the officer on duty.

As soon as she entered his office, he examined her desperately slowly from head to toe.

"What's wrong with you, miss?" He asked her with irony that broke glass.

"I want to report the disappearance of my friend," she replied with eyes swollen from crying.

"You all, that you are going through," he told her, belittling her. "Give your and your friend's information to the police officer, and if we have news, we'll let you know.

The officer's inappropriate behavior left Hope a pillar of salt. She said nothing. She picked up her things and went with her head bowed.

She went back to the police station a few days later. The same officer, with a smirk, asked her again:

"What job did you do, did we say? Oh yes, at the bar. Did she get a little too carried away with some customers?"

"What can I say, sir? I thought, at least, you would value human life. I guess I was wrong." She left, closing that door for good.

The days passed with a heavy sense of loss of the

person who had shared her life for so long. Settled in the house of the missing Lina, she waited in vain for some news. She had made a few phone calls from her friend's phone book to various acquaintances, in case they knew anything. The answers were disappointing: I don't know; it's been a while since I heard from her; don't look for her; it was heard in the street that she had disappeared; and other such things. And as if that weren't enough, she had often noticed a car parked a little further from the house, watching her not discreetly, but openly.

One afternoon, the parked car was there again. Hope was walking quickly on the opposite sidewalk, aiming to reach the kiosk that was a little further down. A man with short hair and a rugged look approached her and grabbed her violently by the arm. It hurt a lot.

"Don't look for Lina, do you hear? Just live your life." Then he clearly got into the car and drove away, spinning.

The Return To The Home Ground

From that day on, her decision was clear. They wouldn't find her. Not if she left first. Would she change her name? Would she burn her papers? But she would definitely disappear. Her body was tired, but her mind was racing like a machine. She was looking at a photo of her with Lina. Both of them were laughing when they started working together at the bar. That night, she had told her: No one may save us, but we will save ourselves. How right Lina was, she thought. It was time to put it into practice.

The light in the bathroom was cold, almost hospital-like.

Another night of pure hell. She stood in front of the

mirror, wearing only an old T-shirt. She had a look that was no longer hers.

She lifted her hair, which until yesterday had fallen loosely to her shoulders. She grabbed the scissors and cut it without hesitation. Every strand that fell to the floor made her feel lighter or emptier.

Then came the dye. A golden color, the color of the sun. Her hands trembled as she spread the dye; not from fear, but from tension. When the transformation was over, her face had changed. She was no longer the Hope of the bar. She was someone else. She thought about changing her name, too. Temporarily, at least. Vasya or Tonia? A name that would remind her of nothing.

She opened her old suitcase. She threw in everything she found in front of her: dresses, loose sweatshirts, dark pants, a hat, and sunglasses. She wanted to go unnoticed. Not to attract any attention, neither admiration nor pity. Only of indifference.

She also took Lina's photo. She tore it in half and kept her own piece. She left the other on the table at home with a piece of paper that read: If you are alive, look for me. You will find me where I began my life.

The next day, at dawn, Hope was up. She turned off the lights and went out into Athens. Another woman. It was still almost dark when Hope sat down on a bench with her suitcase wedged between her legs. Her heart was beating slowly but deeply, like a drum before battle. She was looking across at the telephone booth.

One word had stuck in her mind: Mother. She still lived in Keratsini with Anna, who was now a full-grown woman and studying at the University.

Time passed, and she couldn't decide. What if someone was watching her? What if they figured out where she went? What if she got them involved?

Hope leaned her head against the wall behind the bench. Her eyes closed for a second. It wasn't sleep, it was sadness, thick like a black cloud.

"Should I tell them? Should I go and stay just for one night? Should I hear a voice that doesn't make me afraid, that calls me by my name, without judging me?"

But then Lina's voice came back to her mind: "Try to calm down. I'll go in your place, I've been there before."

She stood up, pulled her hat down lower, and headed for the bus.

She won't get them into trouble. She'll ride out the storm alone. She'll contact them when everything is over.

Walking towards the bus stop, the image of Nikolas came to her mind. Could he help her? But again, it didn't sit well with her. She had been on the verge of contacting him for three years. It wasn't very ethical. At least she could keep that.

Mani, she thought. The village, a past that hurts, but also a potential redemption. A return there might be a return to wounds, perhaps a harsh choice of survival. Eternal memories came to Hope's mind, scaring her to death. She had been born there. There she had learned what it meant not to fit in.

And yet, Mani was the only place where perhaps no one would look for her. A place that had written her off, before she even became a woman. If you can stand yourself there, no one will remember you, she mused to herself. If she went, it wouldn't be to reconcile. It would be to disappear, like salt in the sea. Areopolis was the most likely solution.

She would start from there; there were bars a little further out of town. She wrapped the job around the fingers of one hand now. She had a few savings, enough for her to get somewhere comfortable. Athens had become much smaller. And the danger was growing. The bus, she learned, would leave at ten in the morning. She was just in time.

With a crumpled ticket, a suitcase, and a name that had cost her everything. Hope. A name she deserved, her mother once said. As much as it hurt, she knew that her name was not just a word.

The mountains of Laconia began to darken on the horizon. And with them, the sad memories. The eyes of relatives who averted their gaze. The cold, disgusted words. The words and violence of her father. But now she was returning, not because she wanted to, but because there was no other way. Whatever awaited her, she had already experienced in Athens, the fear, the violence, the prostitution, the darkness. She had even seen death pass by her. Now, all she wanted was to stay alive. She looked out the window, but she saw no roads. Fleeting, illusory images dominated. She saw stones, thorns, and a scorching sun on stone towers. It was past six when the bus made its final stop in Areopolis. Mani welcomed her with stone and silence. The air smelled of sage and damp earth. Few people were on the streets.

A grocery store on one side of the street was open. Hope approached it hesitantly, dragging her small suitcase. A stall of abandoned vegetables dominated the entrance. She stopped timidly at the door.

"Please, is anyone here?" She called, perhaps a little louder than he should have.

"What do you want?" A deep, bass male voice came from somewhere in the background.

"I would like to ask something. Do you know if there is anywhere I can stay? A hotel, perhaps?"

She had been gone for about ten years, but almost nothing had changed. The shopkeeper got up with difficulty from the chair, which groaned under his weight. He must have been close to seventy and sunburned, with thick fingers full of calluses. He was wearing a faded cap, which he took off as soon as he saw Hope to scratch his head.

"Where are you from?" he asked her.

"From Athens. I want to find somewhere to stay. Can you help?"

"Of those, how did you say... hotels... we don't have any. There are rooms down here where the naked people stay in the summer. I think Mrs. Panagiota is there. Go and see."

"Thank you, sir. I'll go."

As she walked through the damp cobblestone streets of Areopolis, she saw herself when she was coming to elementary school, holding Anna by her little hand. She remembered the difficult moments when she received a series of rejections from her classmates. The images that only brought her sadness and melancholy were quickly falling apart.

She found Mrs. Panagiota's house easily. It was not easy to get along with her. Dozens of questions without answers. She told her a bunch of lies to avoid her—no wonder the older woman wouldn't put it down. After a while, she finally gave her the magic key. With a sigh of relief, she took it and hid in the ground-floor room. She had no plan. She just had a need. She would stay there, at least until she found a job. She knew there were a few bars in the area. She left it for the next day. She was too tired to do it now.

The first bar she visited, she immediately rejected; it was shabby and tucked away on a dirt road; God knows if they would have cornered you there if you had managed to get back. The second was called 'The Meeting'. This one was neat—just a few hundred meters before the city.

Inside, red lights and faded vinyl record covers dominated the walls. Behind the bar, a man in his fifties was chatting with a barmaid in her forties. He had a scruffy beard and thick hands from working in the fields. As soon as she entered the bar, he stopped the conversation and looked at her curiously.

"Do you want something?" he asked her.

"I want to work. I know from drinks. I've worked in Athens, a little bit in Exarcheia, and a little bit in Pagrati."

"What brings you down here?"

"Something personal. I wouldn't like to discuss it right now."

He didn't push her. He looked at her again, more relaxed. He didn't ask anything else.

"Come early tomorrow night, and we'll see. If you're okay, you'll stay."

Hope was lucky. As she left, she raised her head high to the sky and whispered, "Thank you!" She was finally smiling after a long time.

The next night, she returned. She was wearing black pants that accentuated her legs and a white shirt. She put on a little lipstick, just enough to make her look more feminine. She didn't do it to impress. It was to remind herself who she was. They talked, they found common ground, and it started.

The first night passed quietly. Three or four locals were drinking beers at a table, and two others at the bar were chatting with the barmaid. Everyone looked at her somewhat warily, drawing their own conclusions.

She arrived every night just before eight, put on an apron, wiped the counter, and turned on the red light on the sign. Lambros didn't say much, but he paid her every Thursday without delay.

The customers were almost always the same. A truck driver who smoked silently at the table near the toilet. A carpenter in a worn jacket who came every Tuesday and drank ouzo. The guys at the table with the beers. Oh, and nothing but local taxi drivers passing by.

No one spoke to her at first, nor did they greet her. They pointed to their glass or raised a finger. That was all. She smiled discreetly, without pushing for acquaintances. She learned to read their rhythm. To give them space. To ask for nothing.

One night, an eighteen-year-old young man, trying to get her attention, said to her:

"You make drinks well. Like the Athenian ones."

He said nothing more. He didn't even ask her name.

The worst thing, after all, is not the insult. It is the absence of any contact. The silence that says: We know what you are, but we will not say it. Like a kind of peaceful condemnation, but a relief, in relation to what Hope had experienced before.

She wondered many times; did it seem she was trans?

One night, Tasos passed by, and an old classmate recognized him immediately. He looked at her through the window; he must not have known her. She knew Dimitros, not Hope.

The 'Meeting' became her space. Not a home, not a homeland. A neutral ground between rejection and acceptance. And for now, that was enough for her.

It was Friday, and surprisingly, the bar was starting to fill up. Two new customers came in just before midnight, almost drunk. The kind of people who laugh louder than necessary to show that they're not afraid of anything. They sat down at the bar.

Hope was wiping glasses when she heard a voice say:

"Look behind the bar, Paul, new blood!"

She stopped. The glass slipped a little in her hand, but it didn't fall.

One of the two, the taller one, approached her. She recognized Paul immediately; he didn't. It was Paul, nicknamed Pavlakas. The other, the shorter one, was

George; he had already put his hand on the back of his friend's chair to lean on.

"What happened, my girl? When did you come to us?"

Hope looked Paul in the eyes, for the first time without fear. He certainly didn't recognize her.

"Will you get a drink, boys? Then the rest," she said calmly, almost politely.

"Pour us two whiskeys, let's see if you serve them well," replied Pavlakas. He and his friend burst out laughing.

Lambros just looked at them. One look, pure ice, was enough. "Her name is Hope," he told them quietly from the corner. "Be careful now."

A pause. The laughter stopped. George whispered something to the other, and they moved away towards the toilet. They didn't leave immediately, but they didn't speak again.

Hope went back and washed her hands. The water was ice cold.

She wiped herself and looked in the mirror. She didn't feel victory, only acceptance.

You can go to the ends of the earth, but some things will follow you.

The only thing that changes is how you handle them. Because, in the end, the only thing you define is your reactions.

CHAPTER SEVEN

WHERE THE LOST BLOOM AGAIN

The Revenge

A winter Saturday night. A cloud of white frost had covered everything that showed life around. The evening, like most nights, was passing boringly. Hope wiped the wet counter with a cloth where two customers who had just left were sitting. Taking advantage of the temporary calm, she then began to dust the bottles and mirrors of the bar with a feather. A glance at the betrayer mirror, behind the bottles, was enough for her to see who was entering the shop, without having to turn around.

When they entered, she didn't even have to turn around. She recognized the voice. Pavlakas always spoke like that, with intensity, with anger. Behind him, George and Nikolos. Perfect!

Hope is no longer Dimitros, but only she knows it.

Pavlakas and his company are now carefree, making a little noise, laughing; they have already had their fill. She greets them politely, serves them quietly, but the inner monologue of the soul is sharp as a blade. She observes them with a smile of hot ice. She wants like a madwoman to set up a game of punishment. The time for payment has come.

Her revenge will not be brutal; it will be patient, almost surgical.

Dimitros is, after all, a ghost of the past. He will present himself at the right moment. Hope is the present. Here she will count on.

She has painstakingly created a new identity that will become her weapon until she brings them to the point she wants to reach. She could reveal their secrets, embarrass them, or turn them against each other. She has known them for fifteen years. So she begins to cleverly tease them, without revealing her old identity.

She gets involved, flirting discreetly, with all three of them. She leaves hints, turns her old weakness into a weapon, and her shame into an art of revenge. With chatty silences and looks like glasses that break in a breath before the whisper, she begins to pull the strings carefully.

Pavlakas, even though he was married with a child, succumbed first to her erotic flirtations. Hope, an artist now, made sure to artfully hide any imperfections that could reveal her true identity in bed.

George, romantic and vulnerable, falls in love as if struck by lightning, struck by the sadness in her eyes. He devoured everything she offered him for the supposedly unfortunate love she had with someone. He moved away to forget, so she told him, and George offered her his shoulder to cry on. Nikolos did not hesitate to respond to her call, either, despite being engaged. Supposedly, the latter was the one who still had all his. At least half of them were taken from him when he surrendered like a repressed rookie into her arms.

The days and months pass. Hope manages to make all three of her pawns believe that they are each the only one in her life. The bar becomes their hangout. In the evenings, they alternately spend time there, hiding their contact with her from each other. Their friendship is shaken. She skillfully isolates them, secretly dates everyone, and drives them crazy. They trust her; she extracts secrets from them and collects them. She sets a condition: they must not talk, or it will at least harm her job; if they do, they will lose her forever. They obey unquestioningly.

Pavlakas wants a divorce. His marriage is about to fall apart. Hope's allure has driven him crazy. To ruin a marriage in Mani? A mess! And yet, they risk it. They see each other secretly at night, usually after work. He gets lost in her love games; she enjoys it and takes revenge. They hide from eyes that are looking for reasons to gossip. In small societies, everyone knows everything about everyone. He asks her, clearly addicted, for the two of them to leave, to go somewhere else, far away; he is ready to blow everything up for her love. She replies with a promise that as soon as the right time comes, they will do it, as long as he is patient.

George, an incurable romantic, had nothing to do with the child of the caves and rocks. After the death of his mother, at eighteen, he fell into depression. It took him some time to recover. Hope recognized his weakness early on and, in a way, became a mother and lover. She let him think that he was everything to her. He lived alone in the village of Sotiras, a few kilometers from Areopolis, in a small house that his father's brother had left him. The only obligation he had was to find a groom for his sister. That's how it is there. Sisters get married first; it is the brother's moral obligation in Mani. But which sister are you talking about now? He saw nothing else but being in Hope's arms and caresses as much as possible.

Nikolos was often away. He was an accountant in Sparta; he came every other Wednesday and on weekends.

He didn't ask for or expect anything from her for the future, except for what he got in the present. It was more than enough for him. Besides, he had a fiancée. Hope's body didn't leave him unmoved at all. The distances helped. The risk of his dishing the dirt on being exposed was decreasing. He was probably the easiest case.

About six months had passed since that foggy Saturday night, and the time had come for her purpose to reach its completion. After this night, she would disappear again. Her suitcase ready, she left in the taxi that would take her to Sparta. She had arranged it; the taxi driver would be waiting for her with the engine running. The appointment with the truck driver who would be waiting for her to go up to Athens together had also been arranged. Everything is planned with mathematical precision. She said nothing to anyone; she would leave, leaving behind shipwrecks and Homeric quarrels. After what would happen, there was no guarantee of what might follow. She would take with her only the satisfaction of the revenge she deserved and some money she had saved working at the 'Meeting'. That was enough.

Besides, a loved one was waiting for her who wouldn't spend a single minute of her life without going to find her.

The clock behind the bar showed ten thirty. It was Saturday again, and she wanted witnesses to what she had planned. The Maniots often spoke of such frivolities.

Hope put on a new red dress. The one that left one shoulder uncovered. Nikolos from Sparta bought it for her a few days ago. He gave it to her the last time he saw her. It emphasized her thin waist with a wide black belt. She was truly a deadly doll that night. She lit a cigarette and took her place behind the bar, determined for anything.

The first to enter was Pavlakas; comfortable, sure of himself, he sat right in front of her with his familiar haughty expression.

"Hi, my baby," he said to her softly, almost in a whisper.

Hope responded with a smile full of promises. The second was George. Noticing his friend's presence, a little shy as he was, he settled for a short:

"Good evening."

Third and always last, Nikolos. Calm, wearing a black coat and a look that weighed everything. The awkwardness between them reached its peak. Three men. Three faces who had once laughed at her. Three people who had hurt her, rejected her, and made fun of her. Now, they desired her. And the worst thing? They wanted her only for themselves. Not even in a nightmare scenario could they have calculated the consequences of their presence there that fateful night.

Hope served them before they could order—whiskey for Pavlakas, red wine for George, vodka with orange for Nikolos.

They looked at each other in amazement, without exchanging a single word. It's a big deal that something is going wrong, but what could it be? Logically, they shouldn't all be here together.

"What's going on here?" Pavlakas asks first with a cardinal's tone.

"What are you doing here?" George replies. "Didn't

you tell me you were going out with your wife today? And you, Nikolos, said you had work and wouldn't go down to Areopolis today."

"Strange," says the clever Nikolos, who snakes surround. "Hope probably invited the three of us here for a reason, but why?"

Hope is serving some customers next to the group of friends, and they ask her to have a drink with them.

"I'll light a fire and come," she replies, winking. She lights a cigarette and, with a slow, seductive step, approaches the three men. Her eyes are glued to them. She stands in front of them. She doesn't say anything yet. She stares at them intently, expressionless.

First, she makes sure all the customers' eyes are on her.

"You were always predictable, boys," she says to them loudly with an ironic smile. "After what will be said, one of you will surely scream, another may want to hit me, and a third may run away in panic. We will see; the sure thing is that all three of you will run away with your tails between your legs. After what happens here today, you will never see me again. Even if you look for me in the devil's hole.

Pavlakas, clearly annoyed, reaches out his hand and grabs her tightly by the wrist, interrupting her.

"What's wrong, Hope?" he asks her.

"It's time to learn patience, my dear," she replies, ironically, abruptly pulling her hand away, freeing it and thus attracting the attention of the other patrons, who are piqued.

Seeing the situation evolving explosively, Lambros approaches to hear the scenario more closely.

Hope has set the scene, holds it tightly in her hands, and brings it to a climax with absolute control. No voices. Just the naked truth, as they never expected. She lights a second cigarette and opens her little blue notebook. She places it in front of them and slowly turns it towards them. She lets them see, to read. She begins to read aloud, too.

On the first page:

February 22: Pavlakas said he would be on a trip. He came to my house at 04.00 am, drunk. He showed me photos of his wife, Maria. He told me he was going to divorce her; he couldn't stand her anymore. On February 25, he asked me to leave here secretly; he wants to live together. He also wants a child with me! How scary!

On the second:

February 17: George told me that our relationship is unique. He was crying. But he was afraid of his friends' reactions. "People don't change. They hide," he said. And he wanted to stop hiding things and hiding. And I would be the one to show him the way to succeed. He can't live without me either.

On the third:

February 3: Nikolos also told me that he loves me. Before he left me, one Wednesday afternoon, he wrote a letter to his brother in front of me, telling him that he wanted to live with me and divorce his fiancée.

The notebook contained many other things, both honest and trustworthy, with so many details that your hair stood on end. First, Pavlakas could not bear to hear any more. He jumped like a spring from the stool he was sitting on. His wounded ego makes him a wild beast. He took the knife out of his pocket.

"What lies are you spreading, fool?" he roars, full of anger. I will slaughter you like a goat, you whore! And he made a move to go towards her.

With a manly gesture, which does not elicit a response, Lambros grabbed his hand, before it became deadly.

"Sit down, Paul. Leave the nonsense; it does not pass here. Put the blade in your pocket, or I will give it to you to eat. What do you want now? Did you do what you did by force? Your ass was looking for it," he told him with eyes that were on fire.

Pavlakas squeezed the knife so hard that his hand bled before putting it back in his pocket. Then he sat back down in his seat, holding his head. He couldn't fit such a disgrace in his mind.

George, embarrassed by everything, tries to run away.

"Sit down, George, I'm not finished. You haven't heard the best yet," Hope shouted to him happily.

Nikolos, stunned, was still trying to understand what was happening.

Hope turned to Pavlakas.

"Can't you stand the truth, Pavlakas? Wait and see what I have for you here!" She takes out a photo from her wallet. She places it on the bar. They recognize Dimitros with surprise. She looks at them. Then, she takes out half of the cut one, which was with Lina. She leaves them ostentatiously next to each other. Hope looks at them one by one and shouts, so that everyone can hear her:

"You made fun of him. She undressed you."

Nikolos stutters, completely lost. He doesn't know where to stand:

"Is this you? Is this you? But how? When? Oh my God!"

Hope looked at him calmly. She smiled at him with a tone of irony.

"Yes, I was. But now, I am the one you see. Don't you remember when I was getting spanked by you?"

"Hey, I was back then..."

"Don't make excuses. No need. I remember the story. But should I tell you? Better this way. You, in turn, without wanting to, helped me become stronger."

Now all three of them see, understand, and remain silent like statues. Not everything fits so easily in people's minds.

"And you know the best thing? I was never yours. You were mine, but you didn't understand that either. Yeah, well, you made your bed, you lie in it."

There is a deathly silence in the bar. Everyone heard, everyone saw.

The next day will hold no secrets. All three left ashamed with their heads bowed.

As they left, Pavlakas stopped at the door and shouted to her:

"We're not done yet, you dirty thing."

"If we meet again, I'm sleeping with you again; maybe I'll have twins!" she replied, with a victorious look and a lighter soul, prompting the patrons to burst out laughing.

In front of everyone's astonished eyes, she nervously puts out her cigarette, takes off her coat, and leaves without taking the photos.

"Thank you, Lambros, for everything," she says to her boss, leaving.

"Wait, Hope, let me get you out. You don't know what might happen to you with them."

"I'm not afraid of them, Lambros. They got what they deserved, and Mani will give them the rest of what they owe. They wouldn't dare do anything, here, now."

Only vindication wanted to keep her company on the return trip. Lambros disobeyed her and accompanied her to the taxi that was waiting for her.

Outside, the wind was blowing, but in the opposite direction.

Some people learn that the truth doesn't take revenge. It just waits for you.

Back To Keratsini

About twenty days after Hope set foot in Mani, she made sure to inform her own people of her whereabouts. She gave Anna information she had hidden from Chiona for obvious reasons. Since then, the two sisters have spoken on the phone at short intervals.

Hope had asked Anna to contact her immediately if any information about Lina's life emerged. One evening, around nine o'clock, after a few months, when hopes of finding Lina had faded, while Hope was organizing her revenge, the phone at the bar where she worked rang.

She informed Lambros about what had happened to her in Athens.

The device was next to him, and he picked up the receiver to answer the call:

"Who is it?

"Good evening, I'm Anna, Hope's sister. Could I speak to her?"

"Just a moment, please."

"Hope, it's for you. It's your sister."

"Thank you, my Lambros," she said, taking the receiver from his hand. "Anna, what's going on? Something's going on for you to be calling at such an hour. Tell me."

"I hung up the phone five minutes ago. Lina called me!"

Hope's legs began to tremble, her mouth went dry, her face lost its color, and a wave of joy and anguish swept over her.

"Hope!" Lambros shouted in his rough voice to bring her to her senses, holding her by the shoulders as he did so.

"I'm okay, Lambros. Thank you."

"What did she say to you, Anna? Is she okay? Where is she?"

"She's okay now. She told me roughly what happened to her. I'll tell you more later. She left you a number to call her at noon tomorrow. Write it down."

That fateful night, when Lina replaced Hope in the detached house in Kolonaki, John, for the knowledge and compliance of the other women of the house, who were perhaps thinking of reacting as Hope, handed her over for free to the customers of his shop, to feast on, as they wished. After those who were there raped her, satisfying their worst perversions, they beat her until she lost consciousness. Then they carried her unconscious, literally dragging her, and threw her onto the railway tracks in Rentis in an old abandoned wagon that was no longer in use. There she would serve the sexual needs of foreigners, at a bargain price, for as long as she was alive; this lasted a few months.

Lina lived day and night in the handcart, on a half-destroyed bed, in the stench of rot and the forgotten. Dirty, exhausted, in a daze of pain, they forcibly gave her drugs to endure. Her pimp, apart from the leftovers of his own food, a little water, and drugs, gave her nothing else. And when, due to deprivation, she begged and pleaded for help, he beat her.

However, her guardian angel, although a little late, finally came in the form of the guard of a guarded crossing that was located a little further away. At dawn one Friday, on his way to his post, he changed his route for the first time. Passing by the dilapidated wagons, he heard her sobbing. Her protector had left her alone for a while, locked in the wagon, and rushed to deposit the night's collection with the big boss. Otherwise, things would have been dark. Without wasting time, the guard, as soon as he reached the post, notified the police via his radio. They, with a well-planned raid on the evening of the same day, caught everyone who had participated in this humiliating prostitution.

Lina was not the only victim in this affair; there were three other girls. But these women were newly arrived foreigners who were cleverly tricked. They fooled them, telling them that they would work in provincial bars, after first promising mountains.

The continuous arrests led to public persons; some were very well-known. The police also dismantled the network of the single-family house in Kolonaki. After John's arrest, many mouths opened uncontrollably and sent him to Korydallos prison for life with severe charges.

When they found her, Lina was in a miserable condition, almost half-dead, without any contact with the environment. Covered in bruises and abrasions, she was rushed to a hospital. She spent about twenty days in intensive care; this helped her in her detoxification efforts, as detoxification began almost simultaneously with her treatment. With time, the support of the nurses and the anguish of her soul as allies, she managed to recover after a few months. When Hope called her, Lina was still in the hospital. The number she had left with Anna was for the nurses' office.

Their hearts were about to break as they spoke. Tears of joy prevented the two women from speaking. How much did they have to tell each other? Now they had all their time ahead of them, and soon they would have much more.

Near dawn, the heavy truck that was transporting her to Athens stopped at one end of the Athens-Lamia highway, just before entering the unloading platforms at the transport agencies in Rentis.

Hope got out of the tall vehicle, after first thanking its driver heartily.

The air in Athens was not the same as that of Mani. It was dirty, stuffy, and sickly. The sun that emerged from Hymettus seemed hazy, inhospitable to her.

She raised her hand to stop a taxi that was passing by.

At her command, the taxi driver stopped at the corner, saying a colorless good morning. He took her suitcase from her hand and put it in the trunk of the car. Hope sat in the back seat.

"Where are we going?" he asked her.

She gave him the address in Keratsini.

The driver nodded, without saying a second word, and started. In her mind, her imagination carved the figures of her mother and sister. They were also waiting for her after so long. She would stay with them for a while; she had missed them so much. Then she would go to the hospital to find Lina, who was now in the final stages of her recovery and would be released in a few days.

When she arrived outside the house and got out of the taxi, she placed her suitcase on the sidewalk. She looked at the second-floor balcony like an old memory. She saw Dimitros staring at the mountain with Anna, and dreaming. She remembered the front door that he had opened for her the last time, that tragic night when she had an appointment with death without knowing it. A tightness in her chest forced her to postpone her journey into memories indefinitely.

I'm here, he thought, that's the main thing; and I'm fine, above all.

She didn't need to ring the bell; her keys were still hanging on the little key ring with the embossed heart that Lina had given her. When she reached the floor, before she could put the key in the door, it opened.

Anna ran first. How much she had grown, but in Hope's eyes, she still looked like that little girl with the shining eyes. She fell into her sister's arms; their hands became knots, their cheeks were wet with those tears that don't ask for words, they want space to flow unhindered.

Chiona stood a little further back, hunched over, with her apron still tied at the waist.

A shadow crossed her face, perhaps from remorse, perhaps from the time that broke the words between them. But she didn't speak. She only opened her arms, and there Hope found her old harbor.

Tight, all three together, mother and two daughters. Like roots that were separated in bad weather and are now entwined again in the soil. No explanation, no apology. Only breaths, heartbeats, and the scent of yesterday's loss.

A light behind their eyelids, warm and innocent. A light that says: We are here, still, with you.

In the apartment in Keratsini, Hope sits at the wooden kitchen table. In front of her, Anna and Chiona. Neither of them speaks for a while. All that can be heard is their breathing and the clock on the wall.

"I hurt you. I know it. I left as if I had never been a child of this house. As if you were not my blood. Sorry for everything. For what I did, for what I didn't say. Sorry for being late to come back," Hope says in a hoarse voice.

Anna approaches her, sits next to her, and takes her hands:

"You were late, but I didn't miss you. You haven't left my mind, nor my heart, for a single day. You are my sister, Hope. And I love you. No matter what happened, no matter what happens. Chiona places her hand on theirs. Her aged eyes are full of tears.

"We all take paths that hurt us. But when your child turns, you don't ask him why. You hold him, you warm him, you tell him: You're home. I lost you once, my child. I won't leave you a second time," Chiona said.

Hope, clearly moved, looks at them both.

"I don't know what awaits me. Where I'm going, everything is fluid. I'm afraid."

"And if you're still afraid, remember that we're here—Mom and me. Whatever life brings, you won't be alone."

Chiona leans down and kisses her forehead.

"The world changes, my daughter, the heart may ache. But the love doesn't go away. And we will always be here for you: your root and your shelter."

And so between words, silences, hugs, and tears, the three women rebuilt their web. Perhaps stronger than ever. Because now, they know what it means to be gone. They know what it means to return.

You don't go around in Mani when such scandals happen. You don't have many choices. Either you kill to clear your name, or you disappear. There are no middle solutions. The company of the three friends had become a broadcast; everything changed for them in one night. Even the sage on Taygetos laughed at their suffering.

Pavlakas withdrew to his father's now deserted village, just before Gerolimenas, Ano Boularioi. There he kept company with jackals and foxes for a long time.

George went to stay with an uncle of his in Nafplio for a few months. He and Pavlakas met a couple of times in the dark to talk things over. As for Nikolos, he decided to leave Mani; he had an uncle who had emigrated to Germany and was going there. His fiancée left him, and so did his office's clients. It was a temporary solution; he would see her again later. He did not lash out at Hope, as Pavlakas and George did. He was overcome by the guilt of his old behavior towards her, and he let it vent inside him. Besides, he had a good time while it lasted.

In the cafés, they could not digest the fiasco. It had become the first topic of discussion and a source of much tension. There were not a few times when those who ridiculed the situation were beaten by those who supported the victims.

You see, there, ever since, anything that sailed amiss would not be taken to the shipyard for repair; they would burn it. The Maniots are a tough bunch—a stubborn people.

For Pavlakas and George, this story would end only if Hope died by their blades. They were not interested in the sequel. All they cared about was clearing their name, both for themselves and for their clan. They had sworn that if they did not clear her, they would not cross the sun of Mani.

Pavlakas had thrown everyone he knew into battle to find Hope. But luck had not been on his side until then. It was as if the earth had swallowed her. The only information he had managed to gather was from a friend of the truck driver who had brought Hope to Athens on that fateful night. So he learned that he had left her at the agencies, and that she was living somewhere in Keratsini. These only.

Luck, however, smiled on him one afternoon, when, disembarking for a while, Sampatis called Chiona from the cafe, saying that he would visit her one of those days. The cafe owner, not wasting his time, made sure that Pavlakas found out. Then he promised a fee to a sleazy cousin of his to serve as Sampatis's shadow discreetly.

So, when Sampatis arrived in Athens the following week, the cousin followed him. That's how he learned the address of Hope's house. With one difference, however, she no longer lived there. He asked around the neighborhood, but no one knew her. A few people knew Dimitros, but he had disappeared as well.

The warm summer was leaving, giving way to the melancholy, hazy autumn.

One afternoon, Hope spoke to Anna on the phone and begged her to put a box on the boat with the samples she needed for the winter orders in her shop. They would keep it open during the winter. Anna gladly wanted to serve her sister, picked up the box from the address her sister gave her, filled in her name and address in Aegina, and started taking it to the boat. As soon as she passed the port gate, opposite Saint Spyridon, where the ships of the Argosaronic Gulf tied up, a heavy man clumsily fell on her. The box slipped from her tired hands and fell to the ground.

"Oh! Excuse me, my lady. How clumsy I am. A thousand apologies," he said to her and bent down to grab the box.

"Aren't you careful, my man? Fortunately, it doesn't contain anything fragile."

"Allow me to retrieve. Let me carry it to where you're taking it.

"No need, I'll take it myself. Give it to me."

Anna, annoyed by his carelessness, almost violently pulled the box from his hands and walked away, muttering. She didn't have time to see his devilish smile. She couldn't imagine that the short time that Pavlakas' spy held the box was enough to find what he had been looking for for so long: Hope's address.

CHAPTER EIGHT

IN THE TWILIGHT ZONE

Hope And Lina In Aegina

That morning gave her a different feeling. She felt something invisible, inexplicable. As if something could happen unexpectedly, and give her joy.

She sensed it early in the morning, from the moment she set foot in Athens. She felt it on the journey back, victorious from Mani.

She had already filled a void; she had built a bridge with her family. What if her eyes were burning tired from the late night, the suffering, and the tension of the last few days? It had become a new beginning, and that was half of everything. That was all that mattered now!

Early in the afternoon, she was standing at the hospital entrance. She was wearing an airy, short floral dress that accentuated her body. In her hand, she held a small, colorful, fragrant bouquet. On the ground floor, she asked the sleepy-looking employee at the information desk which room she would find her friend in. Lina was on the second floor, in room 26. She went up the stairs. She wanted to give herself time; she wanted to be ready for this meeting. So much had happened, so much time had passed.

Lina, thin, unrecognizable, worn out, weak, with huge dark circles under her expressive eyes, but alive. The sound of the doorknob made her slowly turn her face towards the door.

As soon as he saw Hope, he immediately put on that smile that had not been tainted for so many years in the night. A smile that was accompanied by two crystal tears, like dew from the first rain of autumn.

The two women remained silent. There were no words. They were lost in the look they exchanged. An invisible chord fused their pieces, like notes that some musician was rewriting from the beginning to make a song. They embraced without speaking. When the senses talk, the words run to hide; they are ashamed.

"I want to leave," Hope finally said. "I want to go somewhere else, to see another sky."

Lina looked at her like a child waking up after a bad dream.

"Yes, I agree. Would you like to go to a city by the sea? Would you like to? Something just came to mind that I think you'll approve of."

Hope sat down gently next to her, there on the edge of the bed. She reached out her hand to tenderly take hers:

"I approve of being wherever you are, wherever that may be." She looked at her with eyes that spoke, silently shouting: Just a bit of patience; in a few days, everything will change.

Lina had a childhood friend, Stergios. He, on the other hand, consciously did not want to undergo operations like his friend. He wanted to be a lover of the female entity that he carried inside his male body. He had lived in Aegina for many years. He had told her that if she ever decided to stay on the island, he could help her. This decision was, in theory, the best thing the two friends could do at this point. It combined the peace they were looking for, without having to move far away from their loved ones.

They left at a sunset that felt like a farewell. They didn't talk much on the boat; they just held hands tightly, as if each other were the other's ticket to the final change. They watched the ship's waters, which looked like white dreams, disappear into the enchanted blue color of the sea. They watched the seagulls that circled skillfully around the small ship, hoping that someone would be kind enough to throw them something, even a small one, from the ready-made snacks sold in the canteen on deck.

Partridge that awaited them was not a bird; it was a small fishing village, with low houses and flower-adorned gardens, filled with colorful geraniums and carnations. It was only seven miles from the city of Aegina. There, they would start again from scratch. There, they would build their own small old house that Lina's friend had given them, free of charge for the time being. There, without noise, without rejection, without darkness. Everyone helped to make it homey. Even Anna came to help.

When they finished the housework, they set out to find a small shop in Aegina, even if it was only a few square meters, but this was more difficult: summer, traffic, and opportunities were challenging to come by. But, fortunately for them, a few days later, a small shop at one end of the market closed before its time. "Discordant characters of the tenants," they said around. The truth is that the two partners who used it fell out. They accused each other of wrongdoing. In the end, they preferred the "consensual divorce". Prudence prevailed in the interests of Hope and Lina! They were left with a few goods - at a low price - that suited what they had in mind to do. They easily found a lease with the owner, and they started.

They would call it 'The Voice of the Winds'. They would sell books, small handmade objects, maybe even small pots with plants. A small corner in a corner of the world that would look like a poem written by the two friends.

In the evenings, they would sit in the small yard of the house that smelled of iodine. Just a few meters below was the old wooden pier, where the fishermen tied their boats. They would talk about what had hurt them, but without anger, as if they were reading stories of others, old versions of themselves. Then they would be silent, letting the stars say what remained unsaid. Because when redemption comes, it never shouts, it whispers.

Although small communities do not readily accept "outsiders", as they are called, surprisingly, the two friends were entirely accepted. Of course, Lina's friend, Stergios, who had lived there for many years and had prepared the ground, played an important role. So they got a slap on the wrist.

They finally opened their small shop in Aegina. All with passion and dreams. All from scratch. But this time, only theirs.

One cloudy morning, in early autumn, the two friends were drinking their coffee sitting at the small kitchen table. A fragrant sea breeze was coming in through the open window. Outside, in the mulberry tree in the yard, cicadas, bored, were trying to start their song: a vain effort. The last two months of summer passed quickly, giving them peace and tranquility. Their shop was doing great business.

They promptly recovered financially, and the future looked bright.

Lina, barely awake, rubbing her sleepy eyes, broke the silence:

"You know, Hope, sometimes I feel like this life we have here, together, doesn't belong to me. I think I'm wearing it on loan so that it will be taken away from me again. And I'm so happy! I don't remember ever being so full."

Hope leaned towards her tenderly.

"I feel that way too sometimes. Maybe it's because for years we were taught to live like strangers. Our bodies were never in harbors, Lina. It was always a ship in a storm. It awakened desires and perversion. Some nights I jump out of nightmares. But then I hear your voice, and I calm down. In the end, I think life didn't find us. We forced it to contain us. We opened doors for ourselves alone. With words, with silences, with stubbornness."

"Yes, but sometimes, in the eyes of others, I become wrong again. A past that never fades. "

"You are not the wrong one, Lina. You are a poem that they never learned to read. It is not your fault that they chose the wrong words."

"I love you, Hope. Not because you stood up for me, but because you listened to me. And you held me where I could no longer hear myself."

"I love you too. But let's leave the love confessions aside, because we also have a shop to open, did you forget?"

"Whatever you say, boss. Let's get ready. The second one pays for the coffee."

They burst out laughing and went to get ready.

The shop was fragrant with the pages of books and the pots of basil. Lina had gone for coffee. Hope was arranging a new shelf with poetry collections when she heard a familiar voice behind her:

"My Hope... you?"

Hope turned around in surprise; for a moment, she became twenty-three years old again with that apron full of threads and pins. It was Argyro, who happened to be passing by and saw her.

She opened his arms and hugged her tightly, literally lifting her into the air!

"Come to see you! What a beautiful woman you have become. And with your own shop? Well done, my dear, I am so happy for you!"

Hope didn't speak; she just smiled like a child being given gifts. She loved Argyro very much then, and she had been like a second mother to her.

"Come sit down and let's talk, Argyro. Wow, only mountains don't meet! Lina will be here, too. Do you remember her?"

Argyro puts her hands on her hips and says to her with pomp, jokingly:

"How can I forget her? Isn't she the girl who took you from me? Of course, I remember her too!"

"It's not her fault; it was my choice."

"I hope it worked out for you, my Hope. Otherwise, I'll get angry!"

They laughed.

Soon, Lina also entered the store, loaded with coffee, water, and sesame buns. Taking care not to spill her coffee on the merchandise, she almost fell on Argyro.

"I know you from somewhere," she said to her. "You remind me of something. Help me, tell me where I know you?"

"Is your name Lina? You shopped at my store for Christmas three or four years ago. Does that mean anything to you?"

Lina opened her mouth four inches.

"You're Argyro! I remembered you."

The three women laughed happily at Lina's reaction.

An unexpected meeting. A person of their own after so long! How beautiful! The praise and compliments started flowing.

In the evening, as soon as they closed the shop, they made an appointment with Argyro at a beachside coffee bar. They are tired, but calm. The intense summer life has almost faded. They sit in two comfortable armchairs, literally next to the sea, and wait for their friend. She arrives proudly, holding a large box of warm donuts!

"They are eaten hot. Now it doesn't have diets; a little indulgence doesn't hurt!

"Wow, what did you do now? It is a blow to the lower body. Do you know how many years I have to eat? I don't even remember!"

"The more you talk, Lina, the less you will eat. Look at Hope, she swallows them unchewed."

A battle of a few minutes with no winner or loser. If we exclude the spilled honey, the empty box, and their swollen stomachs, everything went excellently.

The waiter came back to take the order. The first time, they didn't order because of the doughnut fight. They ordered two white wines, one red, and a five-liter bottle of water! Argyro, rubbing her swollen stomach, said to Hope:

"You know, someone came and asked for you about a month ago. Probably a foreigner. Tough look, my child. He said your name as if he knew you. He asked me to tell him where you were. I told him I haven't seen you in years. He said he'd come by again."

A vein in Hope's neck hardened. The lights around her dimmed. That icy voice. Those hands. That alley. Everything in front of her again, here.

"Describe him to me, Argyro. What was he like?"

"You wouldn't call him tall, very stocky with shaved hair. He limped a little."

"Don't say anything to him, please, Argyro, if he comes again. You don't know me. You've never seen me since I left."

Argyro, who didn't know what had happened to her, looked at her in confusion.

"Something terrible probably happened to you with him, right?"

"Yes, I can't tell you anything now, at least not here. Some other time, please. Forgive me."

"I didn't know. I'm sorry."

Hope didn't answer. She looked at her and took the chilled wine in her trembling fingers. Lina reached out and gently touched her arm.

"Don't be discouraged, my Hope, it's a shadow from the past. Besides, you're not alone anymore, have you forgotten?"

She looked at her friend with gratitude:

"I know, my Lina. And that's why I won't hide. No, not this time."

Fortunately, this threatening shadow disappeared on its own a little later. They learned that Christos' brother had been arrested for pimping, blackmail, and theft.

In a few days, Argyro left for Athens. The previous night, the three of them had fun, feasting, laughing, and dancing. A small piece of life that they had been deprived of, they took it into their own hands after a long time, to turn it into a beautiful memory. They promised Argyro, as they said goodbye to her, that they would spend the coming Christmas with her in Athens.

Slowly, as the days passed, one by one, the shops closed. Five or six were left open because they belonged to locals who kept them open during the winter. One of them was 'The Voice of the Winds'. Not that it would have any income worth it; only, for the sake of contact, they would have an incentive to leave the house. The taverns, the bars, the cafes were deserted.

They bought a used motorbike at a bargain price, one of those that tourists rent in the summer to go here and there. Its owner was a friend of Stergios and gave them a reasonable price. In fact, he even gave them two helmets. Lina, who had a license, always drove it. The buses stopped running after October, and because they closed the shop at will, the motorbike untied their hands.

At the end of November, the weather was unstable, and melancholy set in. There were days when they didn't even go to the store. A little rain, a little humidity, kept them away. They enjoyed the warmth of their little house on the beach, with the company of a book, the view of their beloved sea, and endless hours of conversations, not about what had passed, but about what they wanted to come.

In the first days of December, they decided to make stylistic changes to their store in preparation for the holidays. To give it a happier, more festive look. Similar to the one they managed to provide, after so much effort to their souls.

Late that afternoon, when they had practically completed their plans, they were both delighted with the result. Hidden lights were discreetly illuminating. Bouquets of mistletoe were scattered around, beautifying the corners. Colorful balls were hanging from the wooden horizontal beams of the old ceiling. Little ribbons were swinging happily, gently at the slightest touch of the wind. Everything was -at least- perfect.

"Our small, our beautiful, our little shop, Lina."

She smiles. She is, however, tired.

"A difficult day... but we did it again, my Hope."

Hope gently wipes the sweat from her forehead and hugs her.

"Yes, but I still feel strange. Something is tightening my stomach."

"It's fear, Hope. The fear that nests deep in our souls. But, where does it end? Everything passes. At some point, we, too, will calm down; life owes us that. So we'll wait."

Instincts do not betray the consequences they predict when you manage to decode them. They are these strange, mysterious sources of messages, which pass from a hidden subconscious to an obvious consciousness. In this way, they want to warn us of something that will happen.

Unfortunately, ignorance leaves us no room for further investigation. And, when what the instinct foretold happens, then we realize that it is already too late.

Hope's instinct took the form of two men. With looks that seemed to drip poison, Pavlakas and George made their appearance. They hated her demonically, she knew it. Literally, she publicly disgraced them. She exposed them, crushed their ego, their manliness. These things are not forgiven in Mani, unless blood is shed. They had been discreetly watching their movements from afar lately. They didn't do it themselves; the person in charge, Pavlakas' cousin, along with another junky he dragged along for company. Little by little, they learned everything. They now knew that the two women lived permanently alone in Perdika and that, at night, they usually returned home with the motorbike. Unwittingly, Anna had betrayed their address when Pavlakas' cousin met her at the port of Piraeus, while she was sending the package to Hope. Whatever they managed to learn, they conveyed to Pavlakas in full detail. So, the time for their long-awaited revenge came.

They set up a deadly ambush on the last sharp bend, just before the last houses of the village. On this bend, for fear of falling, the girls always slowed.

Like a Grim Reaper, ready to take souls, Pavlakas suddenly leaps out of the darkness first. He remained hidden behind a holly tree for a while, with a concrete rod in his hand. As soon as Lina slowed down, before she could react, he drove the stick vertically through the spokes of the front wheel.

"What the hell?" Lina shouts, falling with Hope from the motorbike.

Before he could say another word, the two dark figures had already emerged from the shadows and were next to them. First came Pavlakas, massive, with an iron rod in his hand. Behind him was George, with a knife whose blade gleamed in the faint moonlight.

"We found you, you fagot! George shouts.

Lina freezes. Hope has recovered from her fall and steps forward.

"Behind me, Lina. The assholes won't take us without a fight, not anymore."

They knew they had no other choice. They knew they would have to fight for their lives once again. And the clash breaks out.

Hope, screaming like a wild animal, grabs a large stone that she finds in front of her and hits Pavlakas hard on the left shoulder. Pavlakas screams in pain, and the rod falls from his hand. The pain, however, is not enough to prevent his rage. He grabs her by the scruff of the neck with his right hand and throws her to the ground like an empty sack. He puts his hand in his pocket, takes out his knife, manages the first blow, and twists the blade into her belly. Hope writhes in pain.

Lina has rushed at George like a beast, holding her helmet with both hands, and with all her strength, she manages to hit him repeatedly on the head. He falls to the ground. Out of the corner of her eye, she sees Paul bending over Hope, ready to finish her off.

"No, you asshole, I won't leave you," she shouts at him and rushes at him like a she-wolf whose child is threatened.

The blade that descends to meet Hope's heart is stopped by Lina's heart. She puts her body between the knife and Hope. Lina no longer moves. There is blood in her mouth. Her pulse silently leaves, disappearing along with her soul.

"No! Lina! No! Not again! Not you," Hope shouts, in a state of amok.

Paul, with this development, is lost somewhere; he wanted to kill someone else, and he kills another person, not that this would stop him. However, he unwittingly gave Hope a few seconds to escape. Next to her on the ground, the iron rod becomes her deadly weapon.

A decisive blow to Paul's head was enough to leave him unconscious. George tries to get up, wipes the blood from his face, groans, gets dizzy, and tries to grab hold of something. Before he can do anything to recover from Lina's blows, something whistles in the air. The iron rod that Hope hurls with all the strength she has left pierces his temple. He collapses dead.

Hope is covered in blood. She kneels exhausted, half-fainting. She whispers Lina's name and then silence.

She wakes up later in the hospital in Aegina. The sounds that touch her ears are distant, muffled, as if a nightmare were holding her. Only her breathing does not hurt. A nurse's voice is heard from above:

"Hope, can you hear me? It's all over. You are safe now, my girl."

She manages to open her eyes with difficulty. The first thing she asks:

"Lina? Tell me, where is my Lina?"

Silence. The nurse's gaze testifies to everything.

Hope's stomach turns to stone. She turns her head and sees only flowers, but not the figure, nor the voice she was expecting. Not Lina. She cried almost silently all night.

And it wasn't just about the pain in her body; it was about the loss, the absence of her friend. She considered herself responsible for the loss of her friend. All night long, she whispered with complaint, with pain in her soul: "Why, my God, does everything I love have to die?"

A local middle-aged man, as he was returning from work in the village, came across the area, seconds after Hope fainted. He immediately called the police. When the patrol car arrived, they arrested Pavlakas, who had begun to recover. He tried to deny everything, but who would believe him?

Hope's wound, fortunately, was indifferent, without danger to her health. The knife blade, fortunately for her, did not touch any vital organs. She returned home the following afternoon. A few days after the usual autopsy, Lina's funeral was scheduled—a modest ceremony in the small cemetery of Perdika. Hope had no intention of leaving Aegina. She wanted Lina near her to continue what they had started together. A few people attended. Some of their own, some customers from the shop. Two trans women from the community who came from Athens, holding a banner: 'You will not silence us' —Anna, Chiona, Argyro, and the inconsolable Stergios.

Everyone was in tears, with their heads down. They liked Lina; she had a good word for everyone. Hope, body completely exhausted and with bandages that appear around her stomach, touches the coffin in her last goodbye. She speaks in a whisper over it: "I promised you life. I owed it to you. I'm sorry I couldn't..."

Pavlakas was sentenced to life imprisonment without mitigation for attempted murder and intentional homicide. The fraudster tried to cover it up. He went on to say that it was a fight that went away, that he defended himself. But the evidence, the forensic report, and above all, Hope's testimony left no room for doubt. Her testimony was a knife in the silence of the room. She said everything from the fact that he went to Mani to the night of the murder. "He didn't try to kill me because I said something wrong. He would kill me simply because I exist," Hope told the jury.

No one knew, except her, who killed George. They blamed it on the forgiven Lina. It was unproven, anyway.

A few months later, the store in Aegina reopens. Not the same, though. Now it is called Lina's Light. Hope chose to continue, not because she forgot, but because she never wants to forget. Anna stayed with her during the first difficult times.

Hope's voice was heavy with crying and constant mourning. Lina lives inside her. In every glass she fills. In every song she hears on the radio.

Some mornings, Hope sits on Lina's bed. She reads old letters that she had never sent to her. Letters she had written for her, when Lina was lost or when she herself was drowning in anguish.

Every day that she passes that road, at the turn, she stops and leaves a flower on the ground. The wound in her soul was deep. But her heart still knew how to fight.

Silence is a sacred space. A place that allows emotions to breathe without shame.

The Psychologist

Time passed, but the pain of Hope's soul did not. April had arrived, five torturous months. She was only twenty-nine, yet she looked at least fifteen years older. The gnawing loss was devouring her every cell insatiably. Unyielding to Chiona's pleas to return to Keratsini, she could not imagine leaving Lina.

Then Stergios took action. Her sleepless guardian, all this time, made sure to be there even when she did not need him. He told her about a psychologist who had a second clinic on the island and could help her. He had also helped him at some point in his life, when the need had exceeded the limits.

She refused. Stergios tried again, giving her examples and situations of people who were saved. After constant pressure, she backed down so as not to upset him, not that she thought she would find redemption through it. However, she asked him, the first time, to beg him to come to the shop so they could meet, and then she would see; this went beyond the known protocols for doctors, but when Stergios asked, the doctor agreed.

One afternoon, he entered Hope's shop. His name was Alexander. A Coincidence? He was around fifty-five. A handsome man. His hair was gray. From the first moment you saw him, his gaze won you over. You could tell, as soon as he looked at you, that he was touching your soul. A clear gaze that left you no room to notice anything else. The wound was the next thing, the thing that didn't count, the thing that, with concise procedures, had a specific expiration date. He was one of those doctors who hold your hand when you think you're losing it, and they do it without fear, as if they had been through the same fire.

He looked at her, not like a doctor would a patient, but like one of his own who cared about him. Hope felt it. And she was scared.

Alexander visited her as a friend whenever his professional time allowed. He never asked her to come to his office. He listened, spoke little, touched little, but when he did, it was as if he wanted to replace everything that was dissolved inside her. He loved from the first moment the purity of her soul and her sensitivity, not that her appearance left him unmoved.

One day, he told her, "Not everyone is cured by medicine. Some need time, or someone who is not afraid of them."

Hope was confused. Her love for Lina was a thread that deeply connected them, and it was cut. One end of the thread had been floating in the air for a long time, unconnected, empty. One night, in her dream, she saw her beloved friend and asked her, "What should I do? I miss you so much. I hurt, do you understand?" Lina did not answer her. She took her hand and pulled her high into the air, where she could see all of Athens, all of Greece. He left her alone to float without falling. Then he reached out and stroked her hair: "My love, you are alive. Be the drop that will water the soil with life. Be love. Do this. Live with all the strength of your soul, not caring if there is a tomorrow. There are no givens, my Hope. Live!"

Hope jumped out of her sleep, drenched in sweat. She

turned on the light on her bedside table. She took a forgotten pack of cigarettes in her hands and took one from inside. She lit it, taking a considerable drag at the same time. The dream was still vivid before her; she could still hear Lina's voice telling her: Live. She felt the cool breeze up there where she was, everything so alive. And somewhere there, between sheets that smelled of memories and anguish, something else was being born. Something stronger than passion. More real than hate. A new form of love. Made of what didn't die.

With a hasty movement, she stubs out the half-finished cigarette in the ashtray. She rests both her hands on the bed and straightens her body.

"I will live. I deserve it. I will live!"

CHAPTER NINE

LOVE HAS NO COLOR

A Different Beginning

Time, even if it passes, does not forget to leave a visible imprint on what it cannot wash away. You never forget what hurt you; you learn to live with it. You know not to be afraid in silence; you deepen the bond with your soul.

With a slow and fragile return, you return, you fight with your limits in a delicate struggle on a tight rope. But, even if the colors and scents of spring trace life again from the beginning, you are afraid to spread your wings, lest they break them again.

Although so many months have passed since Lina's death, Hope still drags grief as an integral part of her. Apparently, she seems calmer, but she is not. The loss is a nail wedged in her heart, which hurts unbearably.

One afternoon in late June, Hope, sitting in the small office of her shop, is leafing through a book of poetry. At that moment, Alexander is 'coincidentally' passing by the narrow alley. He stops at the entrance, observes her, and listens to her. He enters quietly like a thief and stands behind her.

"Ritsos? Nice choice!"

Hope, absent-minded, does not understand him; she is slightly frightened. With an awkward smile, she replies:

"It's been a while since I opened a book. I don't know why I decided to do it; it's been a while since I last read anything. I don't know why I'm doing it. To forget or to remember?"

Alexander responds to her smile, giving her a faint one of his own:

"Some words bring back pieces of ourselves. Pieces that we thought were lost."

They remain silent for a while, between the shelves and the scent of the pages. Hope holds the book tightly. He looks at her with admiration, trying to stay calm. He himself knows that the feeling that is born within him for Hope may not be mutual, but he cannot ignore it.

"Today, Alexander, I was not scared by the silence in my house. I made the breakthrough; after a long time, I put on some music. I even managed to cook. You are not saying that lightly.

"Finally, here is a big step. Well done, Hope. It is an act of self-care."

Lately, the two of them have come closer. There was a deep connection that, over time, helped them find more and more points of contact. Hope initially rejected Dr. Alexander before she even met him. However, she accepted the person Alexander from the very first moment. On her own initiative, when she realized the psychological support she was receiving from him, she asked him to start sessions at his office.

One quiet evening, he is sitting in his armchair. On the desk in front of him is a notepad. He is holding a cup of tea that has cooled.

Hope sits huddled on the doctor's couch across from him. She also holds a cup of tea. She stares at him for a few seconds. It looks like she wants to say something to him. Finally, overcoming her procrastination, she speaks:

"I feel closer to you as time goes by, Alexander. I don't know if I'm crossing any boundaries, but that's how I feel.

"There are connections, Hope, that don't ask for permission. They only want respect.

"You know, I dreamed of Lina again, but this time she wasn't sad; she was smiling at me. It was as if she was telling me: You deserve to breathe again."

"Maybe that was exactly it. Nothing more or less. Keep it."

"Yes. That's what I'll do."

Alexander notes in his notebook, without Hope being able to read.

'She is fragile. But in her gaze, every now and then, something unspeakably brave appears. Perhaps the light her friend left her with. Perhaps something of hers that she has not yet discovered.

"Do you want to continue somewhere outside? It is a beautiful evening!" he suddenly tells her.

She looks at him awkwardly at first, then, with determination, she gets up abruptly from the sofa and slings her bag over her shoulder.

"Come on, I will still wait for you? I am ready!" She answers him, laughing.

They walked side by side, at first without speaking. After the first few minutes had passed, Hope broke the silence.

"How much I love this breeze that blows, it reminds me of Mani, when I was sitting on the old pier with my friends, splashing our feet in the sea."

"Memories that are worth remembering are not lost

from our souls, my Hope. They become an invisible force that subconsciously pushes us to look for similar ones in our lives. Beautiful memories nourish us; they give us peace."

Soon they arrived at a ruined place that the locals said had once been a sanatorium. Now it is a place with crumbling walls, full of beautiful scents and wild flowers.

"Souls used to cry here. Now even the stones bloom," he told her.

"I think I understand the implication, Alexander.

"I was sure of it, Hope."

"Do you want to sit near me for a while?"

"Thank you, my dear, but where?"

"Here, on this stone. It may not be big, but I think it will fit us."

"I hope I am not in danger here in the wilderness, am I?" he tells her with a healthy dose of humor and cunning.

"Ah! I don't know; you brought me. Half your fault!"

They both laughed. The next moment, accompanied by the monotonous chirping of the scops-owl and the soft rustling of the leaves, Hope placed Alexander's hand between hers.

"I want to talk to you, not as your patient, but as a human being. I told you what killed me, but I haven't told you what kept me alive. You are that, Alexander. Not because you are a psychologist. Not because you listen to me. But because when you look at me, you don't see my past. You see who I can be. And that makes me want to live."

He put his other hand in hers. Not like a man who wants to conquer her. But like a soul that can fearlessly recognize the image in its mirror. What he felt for Hope was not fire. It was something slower, it was like the rain that falls quietly and waters the soil that has been dead for years. He kissed her calmly, without pretension, but with respect, as those who know what it means to lose something precious kiss. And Hope closed her eyes. And she felt that, perhaps for the first time, she did not need to escape. She could stay, she could set herself free. Hope found what everyone is looking for: Herself.

The love between them was a blazing silence. A breath that was held a little longer in tired lungs. There are times when love doesn't wait for the right moments. It is built from mistakes. In his gaze, Hope found a sea that did not scare her. It called her.

It wasn't always easy. There were moments when Hope retreated, when the pain of losing Lina choked her again. And then Alexander became her refuge again. He showed her that someone would be there, no matter what. Hope never forgot Lina, nor the pain, nor the wounds. But with Alexander, she learned that there is love that doesn't hurt, doesn't demand; love that heals.

"You can talk to me about everything that hurts you," he told her one day.

And she, without wanting to, started talking to him about everything. Not just about Lina's death. But also about herself. About the violence she had received. The rejection, the guilt. The hunger for a hug that, whenever she found it, was lost in death.

He listened. And he ached with her. Without cutting her off, without judging her, without correcting her. And thus, their love found healing, and the light dispelled the shadows. Togetherness was born, as she had never known it before.

Social Rejection

In September, a letter invited Alexander to take over the management of a well-known private hospital in Athens. This call came uninvited to overturn their plans for the future. They had two options. The first was for Hope to leave Aegina, with all that this entailed, and for them to move to Athens. The second was for her to remain there, and for only Alexander to be transferred. In the second case, the time they would have to be together would necessarily be much shorter. Perhaps some weekends, and that with conditions.

Finally, they decided together to move to Athens. This position was a lifelong dream for him. Hope would never deprive him of it. With concise procedures and heartache, she easily sold her shop. She left a legacy to his new owner: apart from the few goods left, the memories that gushed from every corner of it. The laughter they had with Lina the first time, when they closed the cash register at night, and saw a little money in their hands after a long time. The teasing, the joy, the creation, and a whole bunch of emotions that this tiny hole in this corner of the earth gave them.

She would keep the house for their little escapes when they needed them.

Alexander was a very wealthy man. In addition to the high income he earned from his profession, he also inherited a vast fortune from his parents. He had never married despite his age. He had no siblings nor close relatives. His love affair with Hope had sparked questions and social commentary in the big leagues of Athens.

After all, it was said about him at the time that he was one of the most sought-after bachelors.

So it was proven that at some point their bond would undoubtedly create problems, at least in their social life.

The last night before they left, they slept at Hope's house. They sat down to drink their morning coffee in the shade of the mulberry tree in the yard. A gentle north wind was blowing, cooling the already cool atmosphere even more. Hope pulled her chair next to Alexander's:

"Do you want me near you, now that I'm a little cold?" she said to him with a mannerism.

"I want you near me no matter what the weather," he answered her with obvious affection.

"I loved Lina in a selfless way, asexual, timeless. You, Alexander, are the love that came when I had stopped looking for it. If violence stole my innocence, you gave me dignity. You didn't save me; you gave me a reason to save myself. And now I know that I am no longer a wound. I am a woman who lives and loves without fear."

"Do you know why I took so long to tell you how I feel? Because I fell in love with a woman who was asking to be saved. I wanted her to bloom. I didn't want to cut you, sew you, give you shape. I wanted to see you take shape on your own."

She smiled at him with love and gratitude, then nestled in his arms.

The next few days were full of running around, moving, arranging, and adjusting, with fatigue having the first say.

Once they finally settled into Alexander's house in Glyfada, a few-day getaway was imperative at all costs, before the burden of obligations trapped them.

A large, privately owned stone house, in the shadow of Mount Parnassos, isolated, surrounded by pine and fir trees. The autumn scents photographed in your soul sensations of other times. A three-day stay there is never enough. But time sadistically demonstrated its bonds. In the middle of October, the fireplace was necessary not to warm them, but to complete the beautiful atmosphere they created.

"I used to come here when I wanted to hear myself, without the noise of others," he told her in a calm voice, as he approached her holding two glasses of red wine in his hands. A smile was born between them. The wind was blowing hard. The fire crackled, noisily disguising its life.

Alexander threw two thick woolen blankets on the floor a short distance from the fireplace. He also placed a carved low table for the glasses and the bottle of expensive wine. He lay down, leaning his back against the sofa.

"Come, lie down here, next to me, he told her." She stood up from the armchair where she had been sitting. He looked at Alexander with a look that asked a lot from him.

She lay down next to him and let her breathing slowly return to normal. She tenderly takes his hand and passes it behind her neck. He looks into her eyes with adoration. He hugs her passionately. He whispers in her ear:

"You will not be alone, my love, not now, not ever."

Beautiful things don't last; if they did, they would lose the value of their beauty. After three dreamy days at their cottage on Parnassos, they returned to Alexander's detached house in Glyfada.

The next day, he would begin working at a well-known private hospital in Athens, taking the position of director of the clinic in his specialty.

He had already visited the place twice. He spoke with his responsible superiors to resolve all issues related to their collaboration. But he hadn't gone alone; he went with Hope. He introduced her as his companion and future wife. Thus, Aeolus's bags were opened. He didn't know it.

Happy, he crosses the hospital corridor at the first light of Monday. He wears the white robe with the distinctive tag hanging on the left. His footsteps echo in the bare, cold corridor.

His face is filled with joy and pride. He knows very well that some people are not at all happy that he took over, and not them.

He is greeted by his secretary, Mrs. Grigoriou, a woman with a stern look who does not hide her feelings. She hands him a sealed envelope.

"Mr. Director, this file is for you. I don't know exactly what the pages in the file might contain. But I assume they are comments and opinions that concern you. They are written by the hospital staff, anonymously and unofficially, of course."

Alexander reads. Indeed, anonymous notes. Allusions. Some talk about an inappropriate personal life or influences incompatible with his role. Some are clearer:

I don't trust a person who lives with... something like that...

He gets angry at the malice that surrounds him.

He monologues to himself: "Five years ago, I would have hidden it. But now, no. Hope is the only part of me that speaks with a clear voice in all this noise."

Alexander entered his office shortly after eight. Sunlight filtered through the blinds and fell on the folders with the patients' names on his desk. He placed the small tape recorder for recording the sessions next to them.

There was a slight rustling outside the door. Obviously, they didn't know he was inside. Three nurses and a social worker were whispering: "Is it possible that this person represents us? I'm sorry, but some standards have to be upheld."

Alexander got up angrily and opened the door.

"Good morning. If you have something to say about me, I'm here. There's no point in discussing it behind closed doors."

They left as if they were being chased, their heads down. No one answered.

But he wasn't the only one who was accepting social disapproval for his choice. On the other hand, Hope. She was dressed in a simple gray dress. She left with the intention of going shopping for something personal, something she had long wanted to do on her own. She took the bus. The journey was short, but full of strange looks. An older man in the vehicle stood up as soon as she sat down next to him. When she got off a little farther down, two girls were looking at her with irony and laughing.

"Now, does that one over there think she's a woman? Look at how she walks," one says to the other. She tried not to let her know she had heard her. She just walked a little faster. A drop of sweat slipped down her forehead that a tear might have joined. Before disrespect, and now disrespect, perhaps of a different kind, but the offering of bitterness, the same.

When Alexander returned home late in the afternoon, he avoided discussing with Hope what had happened to him in the hospital. She didn't mention anything about her own incident either. Surely both of their minds were traveling to the summer months, to the carefree days of Aegina when they were invisible, even to themselves.

They accompanied their meal with wine a little later. But wine loosens the tongue.

With one hand holding the glass and the other Hope's hand, Alexander bursts out:

"I won't let them break us. We don't owe anyone an explanation."

"I understood that something was happening to you. But I don't want them to hurt you. I can't bear to be the reason you lose what you're building," Hope answers him calmly.

"If I build anything without you, they're not worth it. Don't ever ask me to stop creating for us. Besides, my personal life doesn't affect my professional judgment. If my loving someone seems like a threat to them, then let them look at their own conscience."

Hope got up from her chair and sat on his knees. She put her arms around his neck and let her lips meet his.

The night was difficult for Alexander. He realized that he would drag out the matter with his partner. However, he would see it through to the end.

When he left, Hope was sleeping. He went like a thief, but he did not want to steal her sleep. Morpheus's embrace was the only one she allowed herself to share besides his.

As soon as he set foot in the hospital, he received a call from the president's secretary. He urgently asked him to come to his office.

The administrative manager and the head of some hospital departments were already in the office.

The atmosphere was icy. The president took the floor on his own initiative:

"Mr. Alexander D., we have no prior history with your personal life; we are making that clear. But the malicious discussions are increasing. And this is bad for our clinic."

"What exactly do you mean?" He replies, pretending not to understand.

The president minced words:

"It is not even a normal relationship, you understand, I think. It creates a negative climate. The employees resent it. Maybe you consider it racist, maybe you are right; however, I am forced to intervene for the smooth functioning of the whole."

Alexander, cutting him off abruptly:

"She is a woman. She is decent. And our relationship is not up for negotiation. I am not ashamed. You should be embarrassed for considering the person I love a threat. For whom? For you? Or for the image you built on hypocrisy?"

No answer. The head avoided his gaze. The president sighed heavily.

"We will be back, doctor. But until then, I would ask you to be as discreet as possible."

Alexander leaves the office. In the corridor leading to his office, the whispers have died down. Only one resident psychologist looks at him and nods respectfully.

Wearing a light autumn dress, Hope decided to go for a walk to the sea. Two steps from their house. She stands on the sand, the wind blowing her hair. Her thoughts travel. She remembers Lina, and that nail is still there. She feels guilty for leaving Aegina; now she is alone, she thinks. She remembers her words: "When they don't see you, see yourself."

She leaves the sea, but tries to maintain her daily life. She stops to buy a gossip newspaper from the well-known neighborhood kiosk. The kiosk owner smiled at her at first. Now, surprisingly, he is a little abrupt and looks away.

"We don't have the newspaper you are looking for," he tells her coldly, while it is right in front of her.

As she walks away, she hears a woman behind her whispering to her friend:

"Here it is, this is the one I was telling you about... the psychologist's. How do they still keep him at his job with such a disgrace?"

Hope doesn't react. She digs her fingers into her flesh. The morning light seems hostile from afar.

The days pass, the comments grow, and things in the hospital go from bad to worse. No, they hadn't dreamed of their lives like this.

Hope woke up early one morning. She made coffee, but left the windows closed. The day was cloudy, heavy like their hearts. Alexander entered the kitchen, tired from another night in which he hadn't been able to sleep.

Before he sat down, there was a knock on the door. A neighbor with whom they usually exchanged a good morning brought him a newspaper, and he gave it to him without saying a word.

Trans and Well-Known Psychologist Scandal in Glyfada.

The well-known psychologist Alexander D., recently appointed to a management position, is alleged to be living with a person of "controversial identity" and to be transferring negative stereotypes to the premises of the hospital. Inmates and employees express concerns...

Alexander dropped the newspaper on the table with a thud. His coffee mug tipped over, and the coffee spilled. Hope didn't speak; she just looked at the headline.

She said softly:

"I've been waiting for this day to come, my love. Why should people change? Everyone thinks that anything different is an illness."

After half an hour, Alexander passes the hospital entrance, angry. He holds the newspaper rolled up in his hand. Everyone avoids looking at him. Only a young psychologist, Catherine, dares to talk to him.

"Not everyone agrees with this. I will come, if necessary, to talk together in public.

"Thank you very much," he told her.

They were waiting for him in the administration office. The letter was already printed:

We regret to inform you that, due to recent developments and in order to protect the institution's reputation, we are ending our collaboration. You will receive legal compensation.

"And the reputation of the truth? Who will protect it?" He doesn't speak, he shouts at them!

No one answered.

He only left the door open a little longer than necessary. So that they would understand that he wasn't going in shame, he was leaving freely.

Hope was waiting for him at the exit. He wanted her with him. Her eyes were red.

"We're done with them here, Hope. The bastards fired me before they even hired me!"

"I'm so sorry, you didn't deserve this," she replies, crying.

He interrupts her abruptly, hugs her:

"I'm not sorry at all, my love. Because now we're starting!"

A Doctor's Office In Paleo Faliro

The discreet sign next to the door on the ground floor of the duplex in Paleo Faliro read: "Psychological Support Clinic Alexander D." The bottom row added: "For those who feel they don't fit in anywhere."

Now Alexander is taking control. He no longer waits for the approval of a system that has devalued him. He defines his own framework in his own space. And this space was made for people like Hope, invisible, wounded, but not weak. Inside, two armchairs, a sofa, and a large mirror on the wall, not for vanity, but for something more substantial: to learn to see themselves, without fear.

In the waiting room, he hung a poster, drawn by hand:

Psychological support for LGBTQ people, adolescents, victims of rejection, loneliness, domestic or social violence.

Hope was there almost every day with him, not as an assistant, but as a co-presence. She discreetly welcomed those waiting and took care of the space.

His first patient was a trans girl, 19 years old, who came shyly with her mother. Her gaze lowered, her body gathered. Just like Hope was at the beginning, Alexander told her:

"I am here to help you decide how you want to stand in the world. And I will stand next to you, not opposite you."

The mother burst into tears, not out of shame, but out of relief. Finally, someone did not see her child as a problem.

Times change, people do not. Two years later, the two of them have dedicated the greater part of themselves to supporting people who had not yet found their identity.

Myrto was 42 years old and worked in a shipping company in a senior position. She had built a professional identity as "Marios". That's how all her colleagues knew her, and that's how she had learned to function. In her personal life, however, she lived as a woman. She felt increasingly trapped in the double role. She felt guilty, isolated, and even had panic attacks. She comes to Alexander in a desperate attempt to understand who she really is and how to 'untangle herself' without ruining her career.

Alexander listens to her with respect and understanding. She gradually learns to open up and show vulnerability, something she had never allowed herself until then.

Christos was 26 years old. He grew up in a very conservative, rural environment. From a young age, he felt different. He had fantasies of wearing women's clothes and living as a woman, but he was very repressed, mainly because of the presence of his father, a strict priest. In recent years, he had been living in Athens and trying to experiment with his identity, but he was overcome by shame. He lived a double life; in the evenings, he went around as "Chloe" in Exarcheia. During the day, he dressed strictly as a man and avoided mirrors.

It was to Alexander that he confided, for the first time, his real name and his desire to live permanently as Chloe. The doctor helped him explore his truth with safety and self-compassion. But the weight of guilt on his thin back was enormous.

In Freatida

They no longer lived in Glyfada. Alexander sold the house there and bought a beautiful penthouse in Freatida. He gave Hope the house WHEN THE WIND BLOWS AGAINSTs as a wedding gift the day after their wedding. A small ceremony in the chapel of Prophet Elias. The two of them, Anna, who was also a maid of honor, Chiona, who sailed on a sea of happiness for her daughter, and five or ten loyal friends. He made her proposal one weekend in Aegina when they went to visit Lina's grave.

They could finally dream; they lived happily. Alexander

was now fifty-eight years old, and she was a thirty-three-year-old lady with refined manners and a solid financial standing. He had no heirs except for some distant cousins. Thus, his fortune essentially passed to Hope. The first thing he did was to help Chiona financially. Her mother still lived with Anna. The years had passed for the tired woman. He stopped her from working at the bakery and rented a beautiful apartment for the two of them somewhere nearby.

They often walked arm in arm, clearly in love, on the excellent route over the rocks of Piraeus, full of gratitude for the life that rewarded them richly on all levels.

CHAPTER TEN

WHEN THE WIND STOPS BLOWING AGAINST

Another Disaster

Tonia is a thirty-three-year-old transvestite originally from Thessaloniki. She usually worked in corners down on Syggrou Avenue, near the Hippodrome. Brightly painted and dressed provocatively, she "served" the appetites of males who preferred this type of erotic satisfaction. Artin, a large, thirty-five-year-old man from Albania, took over her protection by threats and violence. A dependent toxic relationship full of extremes and fear. Her very life often depended on his mood. Tonia accidentally learns from a friend about the existence of Alexander's office and decides to visit him in secret from Artin. She desperately wants to escape from him, to be saved, and to live.

With cheap excuses and pretenses lest he discover her, she secretly begins to have sessions with him some afternoons, when he would usually be sleeping.

With the doctor's active presence, patience, and understanding, and Hope's, the results soon became visible in her thinking, behavior, and daily life.

She had a dream that she sought from the depths of her soul to realize; she wanted to escape, to undergo gender reassignment, to live as she wished. Whatever money she collected from her clients, Artin took it. With him in her life, there was no way she would achieve anything. But as time passed, Artin began to feel uneasy. He saw that something was wrong with her behavior.

She learned cunningly from a 'colleague' of hers about the visits he makes. He beat her, tortured her.

Tonia was forced to tell him about Alexander and Hope. He didn't believe her; he thought something else was going on between them. For him, she was the goose that laid the golden egg. There was no way he was going to let it go like this. He threatened her to stop, he beat her, and he told her that he would kill them both. She, although terrified, continued to see them.

One night, Artin went through the street to collect the money. He didn't find her. He became a beast, driven by anger and jealousy. He looked for her in all their hangouts, to no avail. Finally, he managed to find the ground-floor address in Paleo Faliro. It wasn't that difficult. Alexander has supported such people; for three years now, he has been very well known.

For two or three afternoons, Artin stood guard in a small café, just above the doctor's office. His gaze resembled that of a hungry wolf waiting for its victim. On the third afternoon, he got lucky.

He saw Tonia enter the small courtyard and ring the front doorbell. After five minutes, he rang the same bell. Hope opened the door for him. Her smile as soon as she saw his form turned into frozen crystal on her lips. She recognized him from Tonia's descriptions. No one was expecting him. He bursts in with force, pushing her with so much force that he pins her to the opposite wall.

"Where is the cocksucker?" He screams furiously, meaning Tonia.

Alexander, hearing the commotion, gets up from his office and goes to open the interior door, just as Artin was about to open it with a strong kick. The door hits Alexander in the head; he collapses to the floor, dazed.

Tonia sees Artin furiously facing her. She trembles with fear in the armchair where he was sitting, opposite the doctor's office. Without thinking, blinded by madness and jealousy, he takes a gun from his pocket. He points it first at Alexander, who was lying unconscious on the floor at his feet. The loud sound of the pistol sent the shivers of death through her—three bullets in cold blood, two in the body, one in the head.

Immediately after, he turns to Tonia:

"I told you, you filthy one, I'll get rid of both of you. You didn't believe me. Go find him now."

His two bullets hit her in the heart.

Hope in the hallway didn't have time to understand what was happening; everything happened in a flash. Artin, covered in blood from someone else's blood, runs towards the exit, stops next to her for a moment, looks at her, doesn't want there to be any witnesses, he turns the gun on her, another bullet, fortunately his last, hits Hope in the left side of the abdomen.

Many passers-by have gathered outside the small courtyard, anxious. As soon as they see him emerge like a furious beast escaping from his prison, they flee in terror. He, running, quickly disappears into the alleys of Paleo Faliro.

Three days later, they locate him and arrest him in an abandoned warehouse in Piraeus. He was arrested before he could escape, thanks to an anonymous phone call to the police. If a girl from the street, a friend of the forgiven Tonia, had not nailed him, he would have managed to escape. A friend of his, a truck driver, had agreed to escort him. He would have hidden him in the back of his truck among the goods destined for Albania.

The doctor's murder shocks public opinion.

The media is raging:

Bloody attack on a psychological support clinic. The victim is the well-known psychologist Alexander D.

Shock in Paleo Faliro - Doctor is murdered during a session!

They present Artin as an "illegal foreign murderer" and Tonia as a "perverted trans person" who led the doctor to his death. On the other hand, they portray Hope as a heroic figure while highlighting Alexander's efforts to support people neglected by society. Interviews with the doctor's former patients are even published, in which they speak with gratitude about him.

Hope felt the bullet. The sound preceded it, then a sharp stab in the left side, like the point of a knife opening the way to oblivion or death. Her body bent down next to the door, in the same corridor where she had met hundreds of wounded souls. In her daze, she placed her left hand on the wound, the blood gushing hotly. She wanted to scream, but her voice wouldn't come out. She only whispered, "Alexander." Then everything went dark.

One More Wound

The rescuers received her in a bad condition. Her blood pressure had dropped dangerously to 6.2. Her pulse was irregular. Her abdomen was swollen from internal bleeding. The bullet had pierced her intestine, torn a part of her spleen, and, after passing by the aorta, stopped in her spine.

The surgeon, Dr. Pavlou, examined her quickly and carefully. Then he motioned to his team, saying:

"Guys, we don't have time, eight minutes at most. We have to stop the bleeding at all costs; we have time for the rest."

The room was filled with eerie sounds. Electrodes, ventilators.

"We're opening her now, give four units of blood."

Her abdomen was open. The surgeon's hands were immersed in her. Her life hung in the balance with every one of his moves.

At some point, the heart slows down and stops.

"Heart stoppage. Adrenaline. Now!"

Hope's body shakes.

"We have a pulse again. We continue. Don't leave her."

Four hours later, she comes out of the recovery room, intubated, in an artificial coma. She was between two worlds. She didn't know if they were dreams or memories.

She saw Alexander smiling at her. She heard the voices of the dead, the voices of the living. It's not your time, my love, Lina's voice stood out. A light. Then darkness again.

Hope woke up with serum in her arm, oxygen in her nose, and a tube in her stomach. The first thing she felt was a weight on her chest. Then, the pain in her stomach, a pain that pierced her all the way to her spine.

When she finally opened her eyes, she was alone in the intensive care room, with a cardiograph counting her heartbeats.

For the first four days, only doctors came, and on the

fifth, a physiotherapist came.

"Hello", she said, "we need to sit down for a while." She paused a moment. "It will hurt. But it's for the best."

"I don't want to," Hope replied with difficulty.

"Do you want to live?"

She got up in tears the first time. She fainted from the pain. The next day, she endured. The incision in her abdomen was twenty-five centimeters, and the stitches were still fresh.

She didn't want to see it, not even in the mirror.

Two weeks passed. She slowly walked, ate, and spoke a little.

The nurses had a deep sympathy for her. Something in her eyes said that she had been through hell, and she turned.

One morning, alone, she went to the bathroom mirror. She lifted her blouse. The scar was there, a witness to Alexander's loss. She didn't cry. They had dried her tears.

During the days that Hope was in a coma, at Chiona's initiative, Alexander's funeral was held in Aegina, in the small cemetery of Perdika. Close to their beloved Lina. She was sure that if Hope had been able to do it, she would have decided the same thing. His burial took place there in almost secret procedures, without noise or journalists.

Opposite To God

Hope stood alone in the living room of Freatida's apartment. The walls smelled of blood and despair. She had no one anymore. The man who supported her in the darkness of collapse was murdered. Lina, who was there in her unexpected tragedy, was murdered. Her own father also murdered her first love. And now what? Now, nothing.

Three deaths in fifteen years. Hope's life resembled a record of mourning. Everything she loved was taken from her.

In the first few days, she didn't leave the house. She didn't even turn on the light. She ate little, talked to herself, and didn't want visitors. The newspapers wrote. The cameras outside the house, set up like ruffians, were waiting for a statement. But her door remained closed, as was her soul. She only let her mother and sister in. However, as soon as they saw her mental decline, they left bitterly.

One night, with her eyes dry from tears, she got up and went to the mirror. She stared at her reflection for a while.

"I can't stand losing people anymore. If I stay here, I'll die," she said to herself.

She left secretly, unnoticed. She erased every trace of herself. She left her mother a letter:

Don't worry about me, you'll hear from me someday. I love you.

She ended up in a nunnery outside Lamia.

She never spoke to anyone about her past. The nuns saw a pain in her eyes that needed no explanation. They let her stay. They didn't ask her who she was.

The days passed in silence, work, and prayer. At first light, Hope would clean the yard. Then she would plant, cook, and dig the soil with reverence. She wanted nothing. She asked for nothing—only peace.

Sometimes, when she wanted to be alone, she would go and sit under an olive tree outside the monastery. On one of its branches, she had tied a black scarf with three knots. "For those who are lost," she would whisper.

Four years passed like this. On the fourth Easter, she sat on the bench opposite the monastery's small church. A girl from the nearby village approached her. She had learned that the 'nun Hope' knew how to listen. Her mother had fallen into a deep depression after the death of her son.

"Will you help my mom?" She asked.

At that moment, Hope's gaze changed. Something woke up inside her. It was still there. Her gift. The need for the other. The flame. Maybe it was time for her to return.

Regeneration

Hope returned to Freatida's apartment after four years of silence.

She did not return to become a heroine. She returned to help people quietly, anonymously. After all, almost no one remembered who the woman with the calm eyes and sad smile was. Time is omni-taming, after all.

The real estate and the financial resources she inherited from Alexander were so large that they allowed her to build a bridge of help for those whose way of life the social guillotine condemned.

They rented an ample space on the third floor for this purpose, down on Syngrou Avenue. The goal? An informal circle of support for people in need. At the entrance to the building, a metal plaque inscribed 'Rebirth' stood.

For several years, people who had been lost, like her, passed through there. Abused people, drowning in guilt and fear. People raised with violence and disrespect. Rebirth provided help without asking for evidence; everything was anonymous. Few knew who was behind it. Anna, now a lawyer, had taken over the legal work. Applications, reintegration programs, and mediation in social services. She was her link with the outside world. Hope pulled the strings in the background, remained invisible, was the voice on the line, the shelter in the night. Nothing mentioned her name, no document, no sign.

In Silence

Five years later, she bought a house in Aegina and moved there permanently. A beautiful house built high up, overlooking the Saronic Sea at her feet.

Chiona, Hope's mother, died quietly one spring morning at the house in Freatida. Old age had begun to slowly fade her body, but her mind remained clear until the end. In her last days, she didn't speak much, only looking out the window at the sea and whispering her daughter's name. She passed away without pain, with a slight smile, as if she had seen something beautiful just before she passed away. Hope didn't have time to say goodbye. She learned of her death from a phone call from her sister. She didn't cry, she just looked sadly at the sky and whispered: "Have a nice trip, mother." Anna handled all the formalities with Nikolas's help.

Nikolas remained in Hope's life until his old age. Hope felt that she had to do something for this man, who had meant so much to her. Without his knowledge, she agreed to have a repair shop renovate his old photo studio. Nikolas was stunned to see the shop owner standing before him, explaining how he had transformed the space.

With Chiona's death, Hope felt she had closed a circle. Apart from the Rebirth, she no longer had any ties to Athens; nothing held her back, only shadows and memories that hurt her. Every morning, she would sit next to Lina's and Alexander's graves and talk to them as if they were still alive. "I came back," she would tell them, "to be near you. Don't be alone." In Aegina, she found a new pulse of life again, silent but steady.

The years passed like water, quietly, silently, as the afternoons flow in Aegina, when there is a light breeze from the sea. Hope had now permanently withdrawn to the house with the unbridled view and the many flowers. Far from the world and the noise of the city. She needed nothing else, only her memories.

In the evenings, she would sit on the veranda with a shawl over her shoulders and look at the stars, as if waiting for an answer. She would think back on her life: the beautiful Alexander, the great love of her youth; Lina, who left her early but left her a piece of her soul; Alexander, the incredible support of her life; and Chiona, who quietly faded away from old age. She would think back on the people she loved, the mistakes, the small victories. She regretted nothing. She had lived.

Whatever was given to her, she had lived. And now, in silence, she had found another form of peace. Now, time was smiling at her. It has definitely ceased to frighten her.

A FEW WORDS ABOUT THE AUTHOR

A FEW WORDS ABOUT THE AUTHOR

Panos Chatzieleftheriou was born and raised in Nikaia, Piraeus. After finishing the third grade of a six-grade high school, he transferred to the Sivitanideios School to study electronics, a profession he never pursued. A restless spirit from a young age, sales soon won him over. In 1987, he joined the insurance industry and was quickly promoted first to Assistant Manager and, a little later, to Agency Manager.

During the years he worked, he attended numerous seminars that mainly concerned the psychology of sales and the implementation of the Management systems MORAX, E.M.I, LIMBRA, etc.

From the age of thirty-five onwards, in parallel with his work, he began to deal with applications of Holistic therapies. He attended various courses in lifelong learning schools, which allowed him to subsequently work as a Holistic Therapist, leaving behind his previous activity. Today, he is exclusively involved in aesthetic acupuncture and bioresonance, and he also writes articles for electronic magazines on holistic-alternative lifestyles.

His first writing attempt is a true story titled "Seven Souls." Seven Souls was released in 2025 and is already a Best Seller in Europe.

"Seven Souls" is already the best seller in Europe.
Released by Oleander Books.

www.ingramcontent.com/pod-product-compliance
Lightning Source LLC
LaVergne TN
LVHW010655110826
845149LV00014B/3096

9786188795419